GAIL'S FAMILY

A SCIFI ALIEN ROMANCE NOVELLA: ICEHOME
BOOK 4

RUBY DIXON

WWW.RUBYDIXON.COM

Cover Design — by Kati Wilde

Edits — by Aquila Editing

❀ Created with Vellum

GAIL'S FAMILY

A SciFi Alien Romance Novella

I've had a full life: wife, mom, divorcee...and then alien property. All of that's changing now that I'm on the ice planet. Here, I'm free again, and I've found love once more. Vaza's older and a widower, but he knows how to make a woman smile both in the furs and out of them.

Everyone around me has a baby in their arms or in their belly, though, and it's hard to be the only one without. I love nothing more than being a mama...and when I hear there's an orphan at the Icehome camp, I want to adopt him. Vaza and I have so much love to give, but will an alien baby love us back?

(Psst! This story does not stand alone. Start with LAUREN'S BARBAR-IAN! You'll be glad you did!)

1

GAIL

"I know change is supposed to be good," Summer babbles as she hands me a rolled-up blanket. "But I mean, I thought you'd stay here. Stick around, you know? I'm pregnant, and Kate is too, and Elly—heck, Elly's just now bathing again, right? And I think that you might be thinking that we don't need you around here, but you'd be wrong, Gail. You're like the team mom...well, except there's no team." She rushes on, heedless of breathing or letting anyone else get a word in edgewise. "Not really. I mean, if there *was* a team, it'd be humans versus sakhui and they'd win because of the obvious height advantage and—"

"Summer," I butt in. "Breathe, girl."

"Right," she says, and takes in a shaky breath. "What I'm trying to say is that we're going to miss you." Her lower lip trembles.

"I know, little mama," I tell her as I stroke the soft fur blanket. It's already been neatly rolled into a long tube so it can be carried efficiently on my backpack. Vaza told me not to pack too much, but I'm also a mom at heart, and I know that you travel prepared.

My heart flutters. Mom. I'm going to be a mom again. Somewhere out there, there's a baby with no mama and no daddy, just waiting to be smothered with love by a new mama. I'm going to be that mama. The thought fills me with so much joy I can scarcely breathe.

Unfortunately, that means abandoning the new little family we've made here, and the girls aren't thrilled. Summer and Kate and Elly are old enough to not need a mother, but I confess to stepping into the "mama" role around them more than I probably should. They're sweet girls, but they're also all half my age and it's automatic for me. They're all happy with their men, and Elly in particular has bloomed under Bek's loving attention. Doesn't mean it's easy to leave them behind.

"I'm going to miss you all, too," I say, giving Summer a gentle smile. "Don't you cry a single tear. If I can fly on a dragon's back to the other beach, that means you can come and visit any time you like."

"It's not exactly the same," Kate says, stroking her kitten's long, silky white fur as she sits down cross-legged on a mat in my hut. "You won't be just a few huts away. We can't call you to see how you're doing or just to talk."

"I know. Trust me, I've thought about all of this." I've thought of nothing else since Vektal and the others returned on dragon-back (of all things) and mentioned that there was an orphaned baby that had arrived with the island tribe. "Everything going through your mind, I've already thought about and thought about."

"But you're still going," Summer says, sniffling.

"I am," I say calmly. "Speaking of Elly, where is she? We're leaving soon."

"She couldn't come." Summer takes a deep breath, a sure indicator that she's about to launch into another torrent of words. I'm not entirely sure how her khui thought she should end up with the quietest guy in the tribe, but they're happy together. I brace myself, waiting for Summer's hurricane of speech, but all she says is, "Elly's sad."

Oh. "I'm sad, too. I'm going to miss her." And it's going to hurt not to say goodbye. I understand it, though. Sometimes you can't look at someone and tell them goodbye with joy in your heart. Makes things tricky to fake it, so you just don't say anything at all.

Or you don't show up to say goodbye.

I think of all the people back on Earth I'd have loved to say goodbye to. My ex-husband. My sisters. My friends. I'd have stopped by my boy's grave to say one final goodbye there. I'm older, though, and I understand what it means to miss out on that sort of thing. Elly's young, and she thinks differently.

I look at the two girls who came to see me off. They're both still so young in my eyes. I love Summer and Kate both, and they're like my own daughters. At the same time, I still feel...alone. Different. I don't fit in with them any more than I do with the older women of the sa-khui tribe. How do I explain to my girls that I feel like an outsider? That of all the humans that have shown up on this ice planet, I'm the only one with a gray hair? Everyone else that was taken from Earth to be a slave was of a similar age—early twenties. They wouldn't understand. To them, we're all in the same situation.

To me, they're all still babies. My son would be about their age, if he'd have lived.

Thinking of Calvin is painful like it always is, the dull ache that settles in my chest and threatens to overwhelm. It's been almost twelve years since he died and it still hurts to think of my smiling boy and the last time I saw him, proudly showing off the piece of paper that was his substitute driver's license until the real one came in the mail. I hate that the real one came four days after his funeral. I hate that the man who swerved into my son's car sobbed as hard as I did at Calvin's funeral. I hate that there's no one to blame except my sweet boy, who was so impatient he had to take his friends out for a spin only to run a red light because, as always, Calvin was impatient.

Today, however, the ache's a little less, I think, the pain more bittersweet. The past doesn't go away, but now there's more to look forward to. There's a baby that needs me.

"It's hard to explain," I say to the girls, because I know they won't understand.

"No, I get it," Kate tells me in a soft voice. The kitten in her hands squirms and she sets it down. It's no bigger than a small dog, all fur and whiskers, and it immediately pounces on a bit of cord and attacks the end. Kate pets its fluffy stub tail as she glances over at me. "You're in a tribe full of pregnant women with no kids of your own. Vaza can't have kids, and you said you can't, either. I know you love children, so I can't imagine this is easy for you, being around all of this. You smile and you're happy, but I've seen the way you look at the babies." She touches her own stomach. "This way, you get to start a family of your own. Is that what it is?"

I steal the bit of cord back from her kitten. "I don't remember this ridiculous little creature's name," I tell her with a laugh, trying to hide my emotions. "But yeah, I guess it's something like that."

She hit the nail on the head. It's not that I'm jealous. I'm truly happy for everyone here. There's not an unkind soul in the village, and I'm especially close to my girls that I was rescued with—Elly, Summer, Brooke and Kate. But there was nothing I loved more than being a mama, and seeing so much joy on other faces makes me feel so empty sometimes.

Seems cruel to end up on a planet full of babies when I can't have one.

If it was up to me, Shaun and I would have had a dozen babies and filled our home with love and smiles. But there was only ever Calvin, and when he was gone, it left a hole in my heart that never healed up. I went on with life, did my job, smiled, but my soul felt dead. I was a good wife to Shaun, and he was a good husband, but things were never the same between us. How could they be after the death of a child? Our only child? I wasn't entirely surprised when, two years after Calvin's death, Shaun wanted a divorce. He'd found someone else, someone that made him happy. In a way, it made me happy, too, because I didn't have to pretend like my baby boy's death hadn't broken me. We divorced, and I kept existing.

Life went on, and I went on with it.

Up until I got captured by aliens, of course.

"I get it," Kate says. "You want to be a mama. I'm just sad that you're moving away."

"I'm sad, too, baby girl," I tell her and reach out to squeeze her hand. "But maybe we can start the first postal service here. You can send me messages and I'll send them back every time Veronica and Ashtar come in this direction. And I'm not leaving all of you behind. Brooke's there with her man."

Kate smiles faintly. "That's right. Maybe I can talk Harrec into going for a visit once you're all settled in and the weather lets up."

Summer just hands me another bundle, and for once she's utterly silent, as if she's afraid that if she starts talking, she'll never stop.

I smile back at Kate, but I don't point out what we all know—the brutal season is beginning, and from what we've been told, the brutal season is one big long snow dump after another. I doubt there'll be much travel back and forth until the worst of it is over, and that'll be months and months from now. Veronica and her man—the strange gold dragon guy—have made noises that the weather's getting worse by the day, and if we don't travel today, we won't be for the rest of the brutal season. It's now or never.

That doesn't change my mind in the slightest, though. The tribe on the beach is new to this planet and full of young women who have no idea what's going on. Just like I shepherded my young girls here into their first days on this planet, I can help those new girls out, too. I'm the only human woman old enough to have some life experience, so I know when to offer help and when to sit back and let them figure things out for themselves. My lover Vaza is from this place and he's needed, too. There'll be lots of hunting and hut-building and fire-making and so many new mouths to feed. We're needed for sure.

My motives aren't completely altruistic, though. I'm aching for a baby. Kate's not wrong. Surrounded by so many families and so much love? So many little smiles and women with rounded bellies? I feel a stab of envy every time someone celebrates a new resonance, or a baby cries in the night. I help out with the kids and with the schooling, and I'm there the moment someone needs a babysitter... but it's not the same.

I thought it was a cruel joke at first that a woman who just went through menopause in the last year or so would end up here. Now, I think I was brought to this planet for a different purpose. Maybe I don't need to carry a baby because there was one waiting for me already.

Vaza's with me on that thought, too. The moment we heard there was a baby with the island tribe, we were on the same page. He immediately began to make plans to leave, and so did I.

I only wish Elly would come to see me off.

She's...a bit more fragile than some of these other girls. Not in size, but in spirit. She's been through so much. Kate and Summer were newly captured when I met them on the slave pens in the space station, waiting to be sold to my next master. Me, I'd already been a slave for a long time. If I had to guess, a couple of years, though it's impossible to tell time anymore. I'd seen and experienced some shit I don't like to think about again, ever. Poor Elly had it the worst, though. She'd been a slave since she was a child, and kept in cages. She struggles, but with Bek's help, she's doing better.

I worry my leaving is going to set her off, but how can I stay when there's a baby waiting for me on the shore?

It seems like all too soon, my bag is full and there's no more reason to delay. I look around the tiny, stone hut. It has a toilet (kind of), a kitchen (kind of) and a nice, comfy area full of furs that's served as my bedroom for the last couple of months while we've been here. It's been home, and one that I've shared with Vaza. It's primitive but still cozy, and I realize I'm trading it out for a cave or a tent on the beach, both of which have no toilets or much privacy. I'm going to miss this place.

But...I'm still going.

I grab my pack and hug Kate and Summer a dozen times. Summer's openly weeping at this point, and Kate looks like she's trying to be strong and failing. She clutches her little puffball of a kitten against her chest and watches me with big, sad eyes. I don't change my mind, though. I smile and lift my pack and head out to say my goodbyes to the rest of the tribe. They'll understand.

Maybe not today, but when they hold their own babies in their arms, they'll get it. They'll realize why I need to go so desperately.

It's icy cold outside, a strong breeze whistling high above the canyon walls. I glance up, but there's no snow on the air as far as I can tell, which means we're flying out today. There won't be many more snow-free days during the brutal season, I'm told, so we're taking this window of opportunity. Vektal, the chief, and his mate Georgie stand with their daughters, talking to Vaza. My mate—I guess we're calling it that right now, though by their standards, we're just pleasure mates—is wearing a thick fur cloak and a long tunic, a hood pulled down to his horned brow. That's more clothing than I think I've ever seen on him, which means it's going to be a cold journey. I hope I dressed warmly enough. I'm wearing three layers of clothing and I have a big fur cloak, but I'm not sure it'll be sufficient. I'm human, and we're more susceptible to the cold despite our cooties. Vaza won't let me freeze, though.

I study the big alien man and do my best not to smile like an idiot. Of all the surprises this new world has had to offer, Vaza is one of the best. By the time I'd arrived here, I was done with men and their bullshit. Dating in my forties wasn't fun. Men either wanted a midlife crisis trophy wife (preferably blonde and with implants) or a quick fuck. I wasn't interested in either one. If I did find that rare guy that wanted a relationship, he wasn't interested in my pain, and I wasn't interested in letting it go. Then, of course, slavery happened, and I learned that there were some truly awful people out there in the universe. I had one slave master that was awful, and he made me learn new things about depravity every day. I was only with him for about two months before he sold me, though, and my next owner was just old and only somewhat perverted. After what I'd been through? Being groped by an old ooli creep was a blessing. He mostly wanted his feet rubbed and to be fawned over, which was easy enough to fake. But romance? Ha.

Then I was sold again, and ended up on the station with Brooke, Elly, Summer and Kate. We were all purchased together and dropped here on this planet.

And from the first moment he saw me, Vaza made me feel special.

Even now, just thinking about it makes me feel warm and gooey inside. I remember him arriving and staring at me, agog. As a human amongst aliens, I've gotten used to such looks. I ignored it as best I could...and then he told everyone that I was the most beautiful creature he'd ever seen.

How can you hate a man that says that upon meeting you? I'm no one's beauty. I'm older, with gray hair and no tits to speak of, and frown lines were forming around my mouth the last time I saw a mirror. Vaza's no spring chicken himself. His body's as hard as any other of these aliens, but there's gray streaking his hair and the lines on his face are a little more pronounced, speaking of his age. Even so, he's strong and outrageously good looking, and the way he devoured me with his eyes made me feel like a pretty young thing instead of a fifty-year-old woman tired of life.

I flirted with him at first, making sure I was sweet and attentive whenever he spoke to me. It started out as insurance. If this was just another form of slavery and I was going to end up serving another master, I needed to hedge my bets. As days bled into nights and no one tried to rape me, whip me, or beat me, and no one enslaved me again, I started to think these people might be serious. That we might be just people here, instead of slaves.

That's when I allowed myself to hope. Maybe this planet was as different as it seemed, and the people here as authentic. Maybe Vaza's heated looks and absurdly passionate words were truth and he really did find me beautiful and graceful and all that jazz. So I allowed him to court me.

Well, let's call a spade a spade—I started sleeping with him.

It wasn't as if I was some shy, blushing thing who'd never had a man before. After being a slave for a few years, sex was just another uncomfortable function a slave was expected to perform, kinda like popping a zit on your froggy master's back that he couldn't quite reach. If it sucked, you tried not to think about it too hard and went on with your life. I figured what the hell, it was more insurance.

But my first time with Vaza...that was different. When he laid me down in the furs the first time and the look on his face was down-right reverent, that made me feel special. And when he put his mouth between my legs and ate pussy like it was going out of style? Well, that made me feel pretty damn special, too. It had been a long damn time since someone had licked me like that, and I admit it won him major brownie points.

The spur helped, too.

Most of all, though, it was how he held me afterward. He just held me close and stroked my skin and thanked me for sharing my body with him. He confessed how lonely he'd been until he saw me, and now he felt like he had hope again.

Somewhere in there, the brick of ice that was my heart thawed a little. And every day with Vaza, it thawed a little more. The man was like a puppy, just enthusiastic and so damn eager to please. He'd bring me small gifts because he was thinking about me—a bead necklace, or some pretty colored seeds. If I mentioned I liked eggs, he'd climb the cliffs all day until he got a dozen of them for me. If I said my foot hurt, he'd rub it for hours and take care of me like I was a princess.

And Vaza liked to talk. After my ex, Shaun, this was new. Shaun didn't like to talk about feelings. He thought it was a man's job to be stoic and silent. Even after we lost Calvin, he never shared how he was feeling. When we went to the grief counselor, he'd just stare mutinously at the wall, his hands folded, and said his thoughts were private. It used to drive me crazy, and then after a while, I got just as silent as him.

Vaza, though, the man has never met a story he didn't like. He talks to me all the time. He tells me about his first mate, Vika, and their son Azak, both of whom are dead. Vika was his mate for many years, but they only had the one son survive. Azak grew to be an adult and fathered a child himself, but both he and the kit (and Vika) died in the khui sickness some time ago. Vaza does what he can to help out with the tribe, but he's been lonely for some time. He, too, feels between things. The other elders are either ancient as hell—like Vadren and old Drenol—or they have families around them, still. He knew he wouldn't resonate when the women arrived, but it didn't mean he didn't try.

Bless his horny little heart. I don't blame the man for trying to get his dick wet. I think he wants a companion more than he wants a bedmate. Because we have sex (and boy do we), but mostly Vaza loves to talk to me. He loves to share his day and dote on me. He loves having a family again, even if it's just me and him.

I get it. In a sense, Vaza's just like me. We might come from planets a billion miles apart and we're not even close to the same species, but I recognize his loneliness.

Somewhere along the way, though, we just sort of fell in love. It's not one of those great, epic love stories where people clash and fall passionately in bed together. We started out with mutual understanding, bonded with some great sex, and we like each other. He's great company, easy on the eyes, and he makes me smile. A woman can't ask for more.

The moment I heard there was an orphaned baby? Vaza met my eyes and nodded. We're so similar in thought that nothing more needs to be said. Of course we'll go and adopt him. Or her. I think it's a him, but I don't even care. I just want a little one to make our family whole again. And I know Vaza's soul. He loves me, but he also loved being a father. He's lost so much in his life and still has so much heart to give.

So here we are.

I blink into the cold air, smiling absently at Vaza. The man's a distraction, but in all the good ways.

As if he senses that my thoughts are full of him, Vaza picks up a rolled bundle at his feet, shakes it out, and then heads to my side. It takes about two seconds before I realize that it's a cloak, and it's for me. "You will not be warm enough, my beauty," he tells me with a flirty smile as he tugs it over my shoulders. "I must protect my female from the elements. Your soft skin will dry out, and when you caress me, it will be like touching Vadren's crusty old feet."

"You had a lot of experience with Vadren's crusty feet?" I ask coyly. Heaven help me, but the man brings out the flirty side in me. I grin at him and let him bundle me up with care, because after years of being a mom and then an estranged ex-wife (and then slave) it's nice to have someone fuss over me for a change.

He tucks the cloak under my chin and then winks at me, a human trait he's picked up quickly. He tilts his head, gesturing at a cluster of people off to the side. "Air-ee-yawn-uh has brought the kits to say goodbye to Miss Shail."

Oh? I've been so lost in my thoughts that I didn't even realize. For the last few months, I've been helping Ariana wrangle the children into something like a school, though we haven't really gotten far past letters and numbers. Now I'm leaving her and she's going to be stuck watching them alone. Ariana's sweet, but a bit high-strung at times, and I worry she won't be able to handle it, especially with her new baby. But there are so many moms in the village that surely she'll get help...

I bite my lip and look at my handsome hunter. "Are we doing the right thing, Vaza?"

"The right thing?"

"There are so many reasons to stay here," I admit, smoothing the front of his cloak so my fingers have something to do. I find a loose knot made of leather ties and absently re-tie it for him. "There won't be real houses on the beach like there are here. No toilets. We'll be starting over. Ariana needs help with the older kids. Elly needs me. Summer and Kate are still new to the tribe and—"

He snags my fingers in his big, warm hand. "I will do whatever you like."

"You're not helping, you big lug." I start to re-tie another knot, even though it doesn't need it.

Vaza chuckles. "Because I wish for you to be happy. We think very similarly and I know how your mind works. Right now, your girls are distressed and so you worry you are disappointing them. Do you wish to stay, then?"

My heart hurts because I feel selfish, even as I speak the truth. "No. I want to go and be that baby's mother."

"And my heart would sing with great joy to have a son or daughter once more. My joy has been overwhelming since you came into my life." He takes my hand in his again and presses it to his chest, under his fur cloak, and my cold knuckles meet warm plating. "It does not matter that this does not sing with resonance. My heart is alive again, and if its song is silent, I do not mind. It sings here," he tells me, and points at his head. "That is all I need."

"You big romantic," I tell him, secretly pleased. "I want this. I want this so much. It's just...hard to say goodbye."

"It is not goodbye forever," he corrects me gently, releasing my hand after giving it a quick kiss on the fingertips. "It is a pause between heartbeats, no more. The snows will ease and we will visit. Hunters will come and visit us. We will come back at some point. We are not leaving home. Home is here."

And he straightens my cloak, emphasizing that I'm his home.

How on earth did this big sexy man stay single all this time? Lord, the women would scoop him up back on Earth. I feel so damn lucky. Of all the women that have been stolen away from Earth, I ended up here with him. I get to have a second chance at love and a family.

Nothing beats that. Nothing.

I tilt my head up and he leans in and kisses me in the smacking, obvious way he does. Vaza is still not a fantastic kisser, even after months of practice. He does other great things with his mouth, though, so I don't mind. It's kind of charming in a way and reminds me that he's not perfect despite his outwardly gorgeous exterior. Plus, teaching him's fun. I swat his ass as I walk away and love that he chuckles, his tail flicking in response.

Then I cry, a lot, because it's time to kiss and hug each waiting child who's come out to see "Miss Gail" go leave. Ariana, bless her sweet heart, brought them all out to say goodbye and it's a thoughtful gesture that leaves me weeping. I love these children and their precious little faces. I love each sticky smile and grubby-fingered hand that reaches for me. The mamas are here, too, and I make sure to whisper to the ones without infants in their arms that Ariana will need help from time to time. I'm sure it's already in the works, but I've been a mama too long to not steer people with a few words here and there. And then I've said goodbye to everyone too quickly, and Vaza and Georgie, Vektal's mate, are putting mittens on the hands of Raashel, Aayla and Rukhar, the children that will be flying dragon-back with us to the other tribe so they can stay with their parents. Little Aayla gives me a cheery smile, Raashel looks ready to pout, and Rukhar is so somber that I go to his side and ruffle his soft hair. "You ready to see your mama and daddy again, little man?"

He nods at me. "My bag is packed."

"Good for you. I'm proud." I beam at him. "I bet your parents will be so excited. I know I'm ready to see everyone."

Rukhar just watches me, and in the distance, the dragon grunts and ruffles his wings like an enormous bird. As I watch, Rukhar steps closer to me, clearly unnerved.

I extend my hand. "You want to ride with Miss Gail on the trip over?" I ask him, smiling. Since there are three children, we're not comfortable letting them sit alone on the journey, not considering that each "seat" on our ride is little more than a person-sized basket with high edges. Vaza will take one child, I'll take one, and Sessah will be taking one. The gangly hunter—newly considered a man as of last brutal season—will be coming with us. I look over and even now, he's being hugged and coddled by his mother Sevvah. He squirms just like any little boy, though, and the expression on his face is that of someone who tolerates but can't wait to escape.

"Yes, please," Rukhar says, so polite, and I squeeze the small hand that slips into mine.

Then there's really no more goodbyes to do. I glance around at the sea of smiling faces, ready to see us off. Some have sent gifts and small presents for family currently with the beach tribe. Others have offered supplies, and everyone is hugging and talking even though we've all said our goodbyes already. Off by her dragon, Veronica is bundled up and stroking Ashtar's enormous golden nose. I try not to stare—it's still hard for me to think that we're riding on a dragon across the mountains and to the beach. Hard for me to think that the cocky, prone-to-nudity golden man turns into this massive creature. But he's got his saddle on and Sessah gives his mother one last hug, and then Vaza looks at me.

"Time to go," I tell Rukhar. "Tonight, you'll be with your mama and daddy."

He smiles up at me and then points off to my side.

I turn...and my heart catches in my throat.

There's my Elly. Her hair is slightly disheveled, her eyes red with tears. Bek is at her side, his hands on her shoulders, and even now I can see she's trembling.

"Oh, Rukhar, baby, give me a moment," I tell the little boy, and then I move to Elly's side as if drawn.

She sniffs hard as I approach, and tears streak down her throat. There's no wind to turn them to ice, but her breath puffs in front of her and she gulps hard, as if she's trying not to lose it. She just stares at me, her heart in her eyes.

And I'm so, so torn.

Of all my girls, Elly's the special one, the fragile one, the one that is strong in all the right ways and weak in all the ones that tear your heart out. It's obvious that she's been ill-used in her past, and she's been a slave for so long that she prefers dirt to human touches. She says nothing as I approach her, but that doesn't surprise me. Elly's always silent, rarely speaking more than a handful of words, ever. I know Bek loves and adores her and I know he's good for her. I know that at his side, she's taking steps towards breaking out of her shell. I worry I'm going to set her back, that losing a stable influence in her life will hurt her and she'll go back to not bathing and shrinking away from the world. I give her a worried smile, trying not to cry. "You came to see me off," I say, trying to sound cheerful even though my heart is breaking all over again.

To my surprise, she reaches out and enfolds me in her skinny arms, hugging me tight.

I hold her close, touching her hair and soothing her as she weeps in my arms, like her mother would have done. "I love you, baby girl," I tell her softly. "You're strong. You've got this."

"I know," she whispers, and to my surprise, she pulls back and smiles hesitantly at me. "I'm...happy for you."

Oh, my heart. I want to hug her again, and again, but I know she won't like that. Already she's pulling away from me and shrinking back against protective Bek, but the smile remains on her face, despite her tears.

A hand lands on my shoulder. "Are you all right?" Vaza asks, solid and sure at my side.

I swipe at my eyes. Damn it, I'm crying, too. But I smile at Elly and turn to look where little Rukhar is waiting, so somber and patient, ready to go to his parents. I think of the orphaned baby on the beach and my arms ache with how empty they are. "I'm ready," I tell Vaza.

And I am. I love this place and these people, but I want to hold a child in my arms again. Not just any child.

My child.

2

GAIL

The flight on dragon-back isn't what I'd call fun. In fact, I'd call it the opposite of fun. There are no seatbelts, so every time the dragon dips or shifts his wings, I feel as if we're about to tumble from the sky. Up high in the clouds it's bitterly cold and no amount of furs can keep the wind out. My face feels chafed by ice after a short period of time, and I worry how the children are handling it. I keep Rukhar occupied by playing I Spy, which is new and exciting to him.

Luckily Veronica has Ashtar land several times during the long journey so we can stretch our legs, make a hasty retreat to the nearest bush for a bathroom break, and re-bundle our furs. I fuss over the children, making sure they're wrapped up even though they feel the cold less than I do, being half sa-khui. They squirm and groan every time I tuck their tunics in and tighten the cords on mittens, and do their best to endure my mothering.

I mother Sessah, too, just because I know his mama Sevvah and I know she'd want that. He endures it with a patient expression and doesn't complain, and that makes me like him just a bit more.

Veronica pulls off her gloves and cups my face, healing the worst of the winter chapping with a quick touch, and then we pile back into our seats again, ready for another round of dragon riding. I marvel at the dragon—Ashtar, I have to think of him as Ashtar and a person—and his massive scales, his delicate, arching wings that are as big as sails on a boat, and the enormous head that nuzzles Veronica non-stop every time we take a break.

The day seems endless, and Rukhar dozes in my arms in the afternoon. I look over at Vaza, across the dragon's neck and shoulder blades, and see that little Aayla is asleep in his arms, drooling on his cloak. I can't turn around and see Sessah and Raashel, but occasionally I hear her chirpy little voice and I suspect she's talking his ear off. Poor patient boy. He's enduring this because of all the pretty young things at the beach. My mama didn't raise no fool, and he's as transparent as glass in his intentions. Every time we've stopped, he's asked Veronica about her friends.

Then Veronica calls out something that's nearly ripped away on the wind. "We're close," she says a second time, louder than the first, and I lean forward, my butt asleep from the bag of supplies I've been sitting on. Sure enough, the endless snow and mountains break up ahead to a vast, bottle-green ocean in the distance. Oh. I'm surprised at how beautiful it is, and a little worried about the column of distant smoke on the edge of the horizon. The island that blew up from the volcano, I remember, where the island tribes used to live. Somehow I didn't think it'd still be smoking, but it is.

Rukhar points, and then Ashtar wheels around in the sky, and I see tiny plumes of smoke in the air. It takes me a moment longer to realize that the dark strip of land at the edge of the water is the beach, because I remember golden sands and blue water, but I'm still thinking like Earth. I shouldn't be. Everything here is its own creature, as well I know. I touch a mitten over my chest, thinking of the khui that's inside me even now, keeping my body healthy. Up ahead, the thick rock of the mountains seems to slice away, and I see squiggling lines that turn into canyons, and then I see the cluster of tents dotting the edges of the canyon walls. Things move and someone raises a spear into the air in greeting.

People.

My heart flutters with excitement. I lean in close to Rukhar's small body. "Almost there," I tell him. "You'll see Mama and Daddy soon."

He doesn't say anything, but I can feel him wiggle with excitement in my lap, and I smile.

Ashtar continues to glide slowly, slowly down to the beach, circling what feels like a hundred times before he arches his wings and gently thumps onto the sand a fair distance away from the village itself. The basket shakes and I make a sound of distress as the entire thing shifts.

"It's okay," Veronica says. "Landings always suck." She reaches out and caresses the dragon's scaly neck, a sweet smile on her face. "You did awesome, babe. So proud of you."

I glance over at the dragon's big, car-sized head, but if he responds, I don't hear it. The baskets shift again, and then Vaza is onto the sand, his feet crunching as he helps Aayla down. In the distance, I see people heading towards us in clusters of two and three. They're too far away for me to recognize faces, but I see a flash of pink hair and can't stop smiling. That'll be Brooke, one of my girls. I can't wait to see her.

Then Vaza's at the side of my basket and I hand him Rukhar before taking his hand and letting him help me down from my seat.

"Papa!" Rukhar bellows before I can even step onto the sand. I watch as his little figure races away to the group, launching himself into the arms of a big man standing in the back. Happy tears come to my eyes as Vaza puts his hands on my waist to steady me and I catch a glimpse of Rukhar being lifted into the air and hugged.

Families are coming together today. This is wonderful.

"How are you feeling, my beauty?" Vaza asks. "Tired?"

"Strangely enough, no." I beam at him and then look curiously at the people approaching. Is one of them bringing my baby? Or is he back at the village? "I'm not tired at all." I'm ready to see my child.

Vaza just chuckles, and I'm pretty sure he knows exactly what I'm thinking. "You should greet the others while I help take the burdens off of Ashtar."

"Oh, okay." I look at Raashel and Aayla, holding hands and watching us. Sessah helps Veronica with some of the straps, and so I tilt my face up so Vaza can give me a quick kiss. "I'll take the girls to Liz and Raahosh while you do that."

He gives me a smacking peck on the mouth and then winks before turning back to the dragon.

"Come on, girls," I say, putting a hand out for Liz's little ones. "Let's go find your mama and daddy, okay?"

"Aayla peed in her pants," Raashel declares as her sister sucks her thumb, looking sad. "She couldn't wait."

"Well now, that's all right. I bet your mama has some fresh

drawers for you," I declare, and take each girl by the hand. "Let's go and say hello to everyone."

"I didn't pee in my pants," Raashel says proudly. "I was a good girl."

"Yes you were," I tell her, because she's at that age. I squeeze Aayla's hand. "But if you had, it would have been okay, too."

"Gail!" a voice cries before Raashel can say anything else. Up ahead, a pink-haired person bounces and waves a hand in the air. "Over here! Gail!"

"Brooke!" I call out, my face hurting from how wide I'm smiling. "It's so good to see you!"

She bounds forward, all energy, and I barely have time to detangle my grip from Aayla and Raashel before Brooke is on me, hugging me tight. I hug her back, making the same squealing noise she is, because I'm just so damn happy to see her. "You look wonderful, baby girl!"

"I am wonderful," she announces, pulling back and beaming at me. "Are you staying here?"

"Well, I'm not going back any time soon," I tell her with a nod over at the dragon. "Not my favorite choice of transportation."

Brooke just giggles. "You need to come meet everyone!"

"That's the plan."

"Aayla's going to pee again," Raashel interrupts, a smug look on her sweet little face.

"No I'm not!" Aayla declares, her lower lip sticking out mutinously.

"Now, now, girls," I say, automatically turning on mama mode. I nod at Brooke. "Let's get these little ones to their parents and then we can catch up."

"Oh, right! Taushen, babe, can you—" She laughs as one big warrior pulls away from the group and jogs back toward the village. "Great minds and all that. I think Raahosh is back at camp glowering at someone, and Liz is too pregnant to get up all the time, she says."

"I bet." I do my best not to stare at some of the newcomers, but hearing that there are strange aliens here and seeing them are two different things entirely. I see a pair of red-skinned men, tall and muscular, watching from a distance. They look dangerous and unfriendly, and it makes me squeeze the girls' hands a little tighter as we walk. Mixed in with the hunters from the old tribe—I see Cashol and Pashov and greet both—are unfamiliar faces. Some of them are bearded and pale, with small horns, and they almost remind me of the old fairy tales with satyrs, especially in their leather and fur leggings. There are others with big horns, bigger than even Vaza's or Vektal's, and then there's a man with four arms, his chest broader than anything I've ever seen. As I watch, someone ahead ripples in color, shifting to become the color of the beach before shifting back to pale blue again.

This is going to take some getting used to.

"So many people here," I murmur to Brooke, smiling and nodding at every pair of eyes that meets mine. There's a lot of young women. Sessah will be thrilled, I think wryly. There's one who looks to maybe be in her thirties, but the rest are still young. That doesn't surprise me—most of the slaves I've met in my run-ins with other aliens are young and pretty and female. I'm not entirely sure why they nabbed me since I'm older than them, but I'll take it as a compliment.

In the distance there's a large fire on the beach and I see a bunch of irregular seats—stones and gigantic pieces of driftwood that pass as benches—around it, most of them filled. A man breaks away from the group and races towards us, and I know even before he arrives from his tall height and twisted horns that it's Raahosh. Aayla and Raashel see him too, and they immediately let go of my hand and stumble forward on the sand. "Papa, Papa!"

My eyes fill with tears as grumpy, unpleasant Raahosh scoops up one girl and then the other, holding them close. I can't help but smile as his lean face lights up and then he turns back to the fire, where a pregnant woman is getting to her feet. I don't mind that I've been forgotten. It's been too long since that family's been together, and I understand Liz's little shriek of joy as her mate brings her girls back to her.

Brooke laughs, linking her arm in mine and watching them. "Liz is going to be so happy. She's been worried about them ever since we arrived. I guess you can't take the mama out even if the kids aren't here."

"You're always a mama," I tell her, and my heart stutters when someone else gets to their feet by the fire. It's a woman, and she's got a large bundle in her arms. At her side, a four-armed alien man gets to his feet, too.

I know who that is.

I know who the bundle in her arms is, and my heart races. Brooke keeps talking, but I no longer hear her words. I'm too focused on the woman and her mate that start to move toward us, and one of the tiny fists that flails from the fur blanket. Oh my goodness. I'm tense and worried and scared and so full of joy I want to burst. How can they give up a sweet baby? How can I take him from them?

How can I not? I want him so much I feel physical pain at the thought of them keeping him. Even though I've told myself to keep my expectations low, I've been dreaming of holding my baby in my arms.

The woman approaches, her mate at her side. They look like a nice couple. She's human, with dark, wavy hair and tanned skin, and her mate is four-armed and massively strong, and he clearly dotes on her judging from his body language. They're both wearing leather and fur tunics that look stiff with how new they are, and as I watch, she jiggles the baby in her arms.

"Are you Gail?" the woman asks, hesitant. "I'm Lauren, and this is K'thar." She looks over at her mate and smiles.

"I'm Gail," I tell them, and my eyes are full of tears even though I can't stop smiling. My heart aches and I can't stop staring at the bundle in her arms. Desperately, I want her to turn him toward me so I can see his face. Her face. I think it's a boy, but I'm not sure. It seemed rude to ask and I never did. It doesn't matter if it's a boy or a girl or a purple people eater, because I'll love it no matter what. "Vaza's helping Ashtar get unsaddled," I manage, my throat choked with tears. "Is that..."

Lauren smiles broadly and takes a step forward. "This is Z'hren, and he needs a mama. Someone told me you might take the job."

"Oh my goodness," I say, putting my arms out for him even as Lauren holds him out to me. "Oh my goodness."

He's big enough to sit up, his head held up proudly as Lauren moves closer and he turns to look at me. Tiny little horns nestle in the thick black hair on his head, and he doesn't have the brow plating or protective armor that Vaza and the other sa-khui do. His little face is fat and round, with chubby jowls like all babies have, and as I watch, he shoves a fist into his mouth, drooling, even as another fist waves in the air. He's got four arms, which I expected, and oddly enough, I find it charmingly adorable.

"How old is he?" I ask, entranced, as Lauren passes him to me. I stagger slightly under his weight because even though he looks like an infant, he's as heavy as any toddler, maybe even heavier. He's a big chunk of a baby.

Lauren looks to K'thar, who scratches at his jaw. "A few moons. His mother died not long after his birth, and a handful of moons before my L'ren came to me."

I have no idea what any of that means, but I don't care. I just smile and coo at the baby, who's gaping at me as all babies do at strangers. "Hi there, little man. I'm Gail," I whisper, and jiggle him in my arms as I settle him on my hip.

He whimpers and puts his arms out for Lauren, clearly not liking me.

"It's ok, Z'hren," Lauren says, smiling and touching the baby's little fist. "He's not great with strangers, but he'll come around. Just give him a little time."

"He's just little. It's new to him," I agree, but I'm already in love with this wonderful little soul in my arms. I love his fat cheeks, his bright eyes, and I even find the way his skin changes colors adorable, flashing between a variety of them as if he's trying to figure out what to change to. He whimpers again and looks up at me when Lauren doesn't take him. I smile encouragingly.

Z'hren opens his mouth and screams in my face, wailing his displeasure at the sight of me.

3

GAIL

*W*e stay with Lauren and K'thar that night, so Z'hren can get used to our presence in his life. Vaza and I brought a tent from Croatoan, but we haven't set it up yet. We want to make sure everyone's comfortable with us and Z'hren first, and we want to make sure his tribe doesn't feel as if we're intruding. We've been welcomed by everyone so far, though, especially the four-armed islanders who call themselves the Strong Arm clan. It seems to be a given that we'll be setting up our tent near theirs, as if we've become part of the tribe simply by arriving. Judging from the fact that there seem to be a few distinct clusters of tents, I'm guessing where you set up shop is very important to them.

So we have beds in Lauren and K'thar's tent, at the far side of the fire. Z'hren sleeps in a fur-filled basket at the foot of our bed, and it takes everything I have not to sit next to him and just stare, watching him sleep. He's beautiful. More beautiful than I'd imagined. I love his chubby blue cheeks, the tiny little horns on his brow, and the sweet curve of his mouth. He's plump despite the fact that they had lean times on the island (according to Lauren), which makes me think he was fed before anyone else was. He seems smart, too, constantly alert and aware of his surroundings...of course I might be biased.

He doesn't like me, though. Every time he sees my face, his mouth screws up and he starts to cry. Vaza can hold him with no complaints. He clings to Lauren and to K'thar. But when I reach for him, I get a frown, a whimper, and then a wail. I tell myself that he just has to get used to me, but even after a full day of holding him, he's no happier with my presence.

It'll just take time.

Vaza pulls me close, wrapping his arms around me. No hanky-panky tonight since we're literally feet away from Lauren and K'thar. In the past I wouldn't mind—heck, I'd gone years without sex. But with Vaza, I like sex again. Hell, I love sex. Not that it was bad before, but a man's enthusiasm (and okay, ridged tongue and spur) can really add to a woman's pleasure. I'm a little disappointed we can't touch tonight, but I tell myself that we'll set up our own tent soon enough, and that Z'hren's comfort comes first.

"Happy?" Vaza murmurs against my brow as he brushes his lips over my skin.

"I am. You?"

"My heart is filled with joy," he admits quietly. "I have been around others and their kits all my life, but I have forgotten what it is like to hold my own. It is a true pleasure, that."

I know what he means. I can't stop thinking about Z'hren or picturing his little face, the way his eyes light up when he sees something he likes. I'm already planning ways to spoil him, clothes to make him, how to phase new foods into his diet, the best way to handle diapers...there's snowcat hide, which tans out to a very soft, easily-washed white hide...my mind is racing and in the best kinds of ways. As Vaza rubs my arm, I look up at him. "Is this hard for you?" I can't help but ask. "You're leaving your tribe behind to stay here with me and the baby."

"This will be a change, but the others are not gone forever. We can visit as often as we like, and I would not be surprised if both tribes did not combine in the future. Even if they do not, though, we are needed here. Vektal has plenty of hunters who know the trails and the land like the backs of their hands. Experienced hunters are very needed here." He looks thoughtful. "The males of this tribe are strong and clever, but I do not think they have ever experienced snow."

"The snow here can be overwhelming," I admit, amused. It's pretty ridiculous to everyone except Vaza and his people, who think it's completely normal to have a massive winter and a very short "summer." "These people seem nice though. Lots of young people."

"Very young," he agrees. "We are the only elders here."

He's right. It didn't occur to me that we would be, but sure enough. Back in the other tribe there were older families, and elders who were so gray that they looked a hundred years old, maybe more. Here, Vaza and I are the crones. Sheesh. I poke his side gently. "There's a lot of pretty young things on this beach, so don't you get a wandering eye on me."

"What do you mean?" He sounds confused.

"It was a joke." Now I feel guilty. Vaza misses some of my sarcasm at times.

"You think I would look at other females? Truly? I already have the most beautiful mate in all of the world. Why would I look at young things?" He sounds bemused. "I have all that I want in my arms right now."

I snuggle in closer. "That is a very good answer." And this is why I love this man, because I know he is a hundred percent telling the truth. It wouldn't occur to him to have a wandering eye if he's committed to me. It's not only ingrained in who he is as a person, but who the sa-khui are as a tribe. I don't have to worry about being the oldest woman here, because in his eyes, I'm his sexy, beautiful mate. There's no such thing as a midlife crisis or a trophy wife.

Just reminds me of how different things are here than on Earth.

I smile into the darkness at Vaza's glowing blue eyes and touch his cheek. Even though it's crowded in this tent, it doesn't mean we can't play a little. I lean in to kiss him, teasing my lips over his, and his hands tighten on my body with excitement.

A fussy cry breaks the silence of the night, and then Z'hren wails his displeasure.

Ah yes, it's been a long time since a baby kept me awake past my bedtime. I don't even mind it, because it reminds me that there's a little one to love. I sit up in bed, reaching for the basket.

"Mmm," Lauren says, and I glance over to see that she's sitting up in her furs, rubbing her glowing eyes. "You want to take him, or you want me to?"

"We've got it," I reassure her. "Go back to sleep."

I reach into the basket and pick up Z'hren, clucking at him. Probably a wet diaper or hungry. He's still little enough that he'll get fussy in the middle of the night without something to eat. "Hi, little man," I whisper to him, pulling him against my body and patting his back. "It's okay."

He blasts my eardrums with an even louder wail, screaming his head off. With four small hands, he pushes away from me, leaning away and acting as if I'm a monster.

"Let me try before he wakes the entire camp," Vaza murmurs, taking Z'hren from my arms. He picks up the heavy child as if he weighs nothing and holds him close, shushing him.

Immediately, the baby's attitude changes. He whimpers, and then gives a fussy hiccup as Vaza rocks him. "His bottom is wet," my man murmurs, and then lays the baby down so he can change him, clucking and murmuring to Z'hren to keep him occupied as little fists wave in the air.

I watch, my smile somewhat guarded as I hand Vaza new wraps and soft bits of fur to clean the child off. I can't deny that I love that Vaza jumps right in to help out with the baby and that he's good with him. Vaza loves children. He's got a kind heart for all of his flirty, lascivious ways, and I think he'd love to be a daddy again. But damn, it hurts that Z'hren can't stand me. Even sleepy and miserable, he doesn't want anything to do with me.

It's hard not to let it affect my mood. I know he's just a baby. I know I'm probably strange to him, but...surely I can't be that bad. Is it all humans he hates or just me? I think of how Z'hren clung to Lauren, and I worry it's really just me.

Z'HREN'S A GOOD BABY. He sleeps almost through the night, and when we wake up the next morning, he's fussy with hunger but quiets once we give him one of the specially made trail ration bars that Lauren's been making for him since they arrived on the beach. They're made with meat that's been pounded and pulped into a paste, fat, and a seed paste, then frozen in a bowl of snow. It's not the ideal way to feed a baby, but as Z'hren gnaws on one happily, I suppose it's as good a diet as pureed peas and carrots.

I change him into fresh clothing, cooing and singing to him as I do. He whimpers uncertainly, and when I pick him up, he automatically reaches for Lauren, and when she doesn't take him, then Vaza.

"He's just adjusting," Lauren says for what feels like the hundredth time since we arrived. She's still encouraging, and Vaza is too. As we head out for breakfast, he takes Z'hren into his arms and tosses the little one in the air. The baby's all giggles and laughter for him.

It's just me he doesn't seem to like. I try not to take it personally. Babies don't like change, and I wonder if it's my smell. He likes Lauren, but she's also resonating to K'thar, her breast humming as she starts her day. Vaza probably smells like familiar people, too. If I smell different and I'm not humming, I'm probably too strange for him.

At least, that's what I tell myself.

"Ho, Vaza," Cashol says, jogging up. "I am going to take the clan of the Tall Horn into the hills and show them how to read a cache. We can bring more people along with us if you come to help out. I know J'shel and K'thar will want to go, as well."

"Me too," Lauren says. "If K'thar's going, I want to go, too. I can learn to hunt."

Vaza's face is bright with excitement. Nothing that man loves more than being needed. I can see it in his eyes, and I want to hug him when he immediately turns to me instead. Thoughtful man.

"You go," I tell him before he can ask. I smile and hold my arms out for Z'hren. "I'll be fine."

"Are you sure?" He hesitates, then hands Z'hren over to me, ignoring the fussing of the baby. "We were going to set up our tent today."

"We can set it up tomorrow," I tell him easily. "Go and hunt. Stretch your legs. I'll get to know this little man," I say, and tap one of Z'hren's fat cheeks.

His lower lip sticks out and he looks as if he's ready to cry. Then, he looks over at Vaza and puts his arms out.

Definitely starting to feel like a leper.

"Go," I tell Vaza, before he can volunteer to stay. "But leave me one of your tunics. He likes your scent more than mine."

4

GAIL

I hang out by the main fire that day, because it's the best way to meet people. I hug both Harlow and Liz, who are thrilled to have their children back, and we catch up on what's going on back at Croatoan—who had babies recently, who resonated again, how friends are doing, and where the kits are on their lessons with Ariana. I find myself chattering away even as Z'hren squirms and fusses in my arms. He's got a strong personality already, my little man, and it'd be cute if his dislike wasn't directed at me.

I meet several of the new girls, too, and almost to a one, they're all young and inexperienced with living in the rougher conditions of this world, so I feel I can help out there. I listen politely as a young lady named Devi chatters my ear off about meteorological weather patterns shaping the ecology here while a very pregnant woman named Angie sits across the fire and pokes at it forlornly.

There are some interesting dynamics in this new tribe, especially given that most of the women are not mated. I notice that whenever a group passes through camp, they stop by the fire to talk to some of the girls. I also notice that Angie has a lot of attention from the two stern-looking red aliens, which is odd. She's pregnant, but it's obvious the daddy didn't get stranded with her, so there's a story there. I don't ask, though. I'm still a stranger. Instead, I listen to Bridget complain about how everyone mispronounces her name, chat with Brooke when she sits down, and watch as Harlow tries to instruct Hannah and Penny on how to clean a dvisti hide that's stretched out on a frame.

Life goes on around us. Despite the fact that there are a lot of new faces here and new aliens, the energy feels very similar to back at Croatoan. There's a spirit of helpfulness, of working together, and I love that. This is a community, for all that there are sly glances between men and women and a current of sexual tension that can't be ignored.

And there's the beach, which is a nice change of pace from the high-walled canyon the Croatoan huts are tucked into. Here, there's fresh air and an ocean breeze, and if the ocean's a little creepy, that's all right. I don't plan on swimming. I just like the view. I like the rocky cliffs that remind me of pictures I once saw of Dover. I like how it's bleak but open, and most of all, I like that the weather here is milder, the snow less blanketing. It's like this little beach cove is isolated from all of the snowstorms that pound the rest of the land.

This is a good place to raise a family.

My day is full of baby-wrangling, and the hours pass before I know it. Taking care of Z'hren reminds me of when my little Calvin had his endless ear infections as a baby. He was constantly fussy and miserable. He didn't want to be held, but didn't want to be put down, either. Everything made him angry, and his wailing and misery followed me constantly. Z'hren is like that, and I can't make him happy. Like Calvin, I know it takes time and patience, but when I see a few sympathetic looks sent my way, I wish that for just five minutes, Z'hren liked me. That he'd quiet down and see how much I love him and want to care for him.

No such luck.

Liz and the girls she's teaching show up at the fire in the afternoon and they chop vegetables and meat to make stew in one of the industrial-sized pouches that serve as cookpots in this place. Raashel helps her mother, and Aayla, well, Aayla gnaws on a vegetable before tossing it into the pile with the others. One of the new girls, Tia, looks appalled, but anyone that's had a baby knows that a little slobber never hurt anything. I take one of the peeled roots and offer it to Z'hren to chew on. Maybe he's teething and that's why he's so miserable all the time.

He takes the root and looks at me, big eyes blinking, and my heart swells with love.

"Hi there," I whisper to him, and I can't stop smiling.

He waves the root in the air, and then his little face breaks into a smile, and I feel pure joy. He's starting to like me. He—

"Hey," Lauren says, coming up from behind. "How's Z'hren behaving?"

As I watch, the baby's gaze follows her and my heart sinks again. That smile wasn't for me. It was for Lauren. Even now, he reaches for her. She just takes his little fist and gives it a jiggle, smiling at him.

"It's been a *day*," I admit, letting my inflection show it hasn't been a great one. "But we're getting there. Is he teething?"

"Teething? Oh, I don't think so? Not yet?" She shrugs and thumps down onto the seat next to me, sweaty and tired. "Boy. I had no idea hunting was so hard. You want me to take him for a bit?"

"No, I'm okay," I tell her, and shift Z'hren on my lap. "Vaza with you?"

"He's showing K'thar how to bleed out the kill. They wanted me to sit down and rest for a bit." She makes a face. "I keep forgetting that I'm pregnant, so whenever I get tired, I get really tired, and K'thar panics." She yawns. "The two of them don't understand that humans don't normally tromp through snow and hunt our food, so of course we're tired. The only thing I've ever hunted is a sale at the grocery store."

Across the fire, someone chuckles in agreement and Lauren flashes a smile in their direction.

Z'hren gnaws on the root, watching Lauren, and I feel a pang of worry. He's clearly attached to her and doesn't like me. Maybe this is a mistake. No matter how much I love him, how can I take him away from Lauren and K'thar? If he was mine, I'd never give him up.

"Is this okay?" I ask her softly, because I have to know.

She straightens and blinks at me. "You taking Z'hren? Of course it's okay. We were the ones that suggested it."

"I know. I can tell you love him, though." And he loves her more than he loves me.

Lauren smiles and reaches out to touch one waving fist. "He's impossible not to love. I'm not sure I'm entirely ready for two babies just yet. K'thar and I are still new, this planet is new, and..." She spreads her hands. "Everything is new. I want a chance to settle in to my relationship and the thought of being a mother. It sounds selfish, I know."

"It's not," I tell her with a smile. "I would never think you're self-ish. Not after what you've done for me and Vaza." And I hug Z'hren a little tighter, even though he fusses.

She smiles at me. "I just think he deserves to be the light of some-one's world."

He will be. "Vaza and I are going to stay here, just so you know. We think Z'hren should be raised around his people. It's only fair."

"That sounds wonderful." And her happy expression is genuine. "I'm glad you two are going to be his parents."

"I didn't realize how much I wanted it until it was offered," I admit. "Then I couldn't stop thinking about it." When Z'hren makes an angry sound, I can't help but ask. "Is he this cranky to everyone?"

"He's not a big fan of strangers," Lauren admits. "I think too much has been changing on him all at once. He's had to deal with a lot of adjustments in a short period of time."

"My poor baby," I murmur, smoothing his hair back from his little horns. "You have, haven't you?" I realize the girls on this beach aren't the only one with their lives upside down lately. Little Z'hren has lost his mama and changed hands, changed homes, changed climates, and I suspect even his diet is different. No wonder he's cranky. His head's probably spinning.

What he needs is stability. It's what all babies need. And Vaza and I can give that to him, I vow. Nothing's more important than Z'hren's comfort right now. If that means he has to scream in my face every day and every night, then that's all right.

I lean in and give his sweet forehead a kiss, and I don't even mind when he pulls away.

Much.

OF COURSE, it's easy to say that you can be patient and kind and understanding when the child in your arms is quiet. It's much harder when, day after day, the child keeps fussing and hating you.

I rock Z'hren to sleep and sing him songs. I play with him on his blankets and make sure he gets plenty of food and naps and his leather-clad bottom is never dirty for longer than a moment. I shower love on him and I let him yell in my face, pull my short hair, and fuss for as long as he needs to. He has a comfy basket at the foot of the bed I share with Vaza, and we finally have a tent of our own set up, nestled amongst the other tents of the Strong Arm clan. They've made us feel welcome and included, and everyone seems happy that we've taken on the role of parenting Z'hren.

Z'hren loves his tribe, too. He coos happily at the sight of N'dek, who spends most of his days by the fire. He plays with J'shel's long, gleaming black braid and always has smiles for Lauren and K'thar. He even loves K'thar's weird little bird pet that sits on his shoulder and shivers in a stiff breeze. The silly thing wears a little fur jacket that Lauren made for him and squawks unpleasantly throughout the day. It also seems to love Z'hren, playing at times in a way like a puppy would with a baby.

And of course Z'hren loves Vaza. He lights up every time my mate picks him up. Vaza's a great daddy, too. He wakes up in the middle of the night when Z'hren's fussing and changes him or rocks him without a complaint. He hunts down eggs when we find that snowcat makes Z'hren's tummy upset. I couldn't ask for a better partner.

Which is why when I have a meltdown in the middle of the night,
I feel like a jerk.

5

GAIL

Z'hren wakes up—as he always does—shortly after Vaza and I go to sleep. He wails, and I pat Vaza's arm.

"I'll get him," I murmur. "You go back to sleep."

Vaza just grunts and rolls over.

I cross the tent in the middle of the night and pick up Z'hren, clucking at him. "Now, now," I murmur, hefting him in my arms. He's a big baby, being fully sa-khui—or sakh, or whatever the island people call themselves. I make a mental note to ask K'thar tomorrow.

Z'hren hiccups, then wails in my face. One little fist smacks into my mouth with surprising force, and my lip splits, bleeding down my chin.

"Shit." I juggle the screaming baby in my arms, mindful of the fact that it's an encampment and when he wakes up, he wakes up everyone. Tonight he's in no mood to be quiet, his voice thunderous with displeasure. I change his furry nappy, swiping at my bleeding, throbbing lip as I do so. "It's all right, little man. Let's not cry, okay?" I murmur, my voice singsong and low like a lullaby. "Let's get you changed and fed and back to sleep, all right?"

He continues screaming, heedless of my words, and flails his little arms furiously.

I pick him up and offer him a snack, which he flings away. I grab one of his favorite roots to gnaw on and hand it to him. It's peeled and ready to go, but he doesn't want it, either. He just wants to cry. I'm so frustrated and tired and defeated that I feel a moment of utter despair.

Vaza gets out of bed, stumbling over to my side. "Let me help, my Shail, before he wakes the entire camp."

"I can do it," I tell him, frustrated, but he takes the baby from my arms despite my protests.

Z'hren hiccups, coughs, and then his crying settles down into nothing as Vaza tucks him under his chin and strokes his back.

It hurts. My lip hurts and my heart hurts and I feel like a monster for a baby to hate me so much for no reason at all. I'm tired and miserable and a baby's been screaming in my face for the past week, and my nerves are shot. I burst into tears, burying my face in my hands and weeping.

"Shail?" Vaza murmurs, astonished. In all the months we've been together, I've never wept like this. Weeping when leaving behind Kate and Summer is different than sobbing out my misery.

But I'm just so...sad. I want this more than anything. I love Z'hren already, and seeing his little face makes my heart light up. I want to be his mama.

He just doesn't want me, and that is utterly crushing.

"I just need a minute," I tell him, trying to compose myself and failing. I'm tired, I'm sad, and most of all, my heart hurts. I haven't done anything to make an infant hate me, but for some reason, he can't get it into his head that I want nothing more than to love him and take care of him. Instead, he screams like I'm killing him every time I approach.

"What is wrong?" Vaza sounds so worried, even as he jiggles the baby, trying to calm his crying. It's a whole tent full of wailing tonight, it seems, and that just makes me feel even worse. I want to help take care of Z'hren, but I don't dare try because if he screams any louder, he's going to wake the entire encampment, not just the Strong Arm clan who is set up nearby. "Shail, speak to me. Tell me why you cry."

"I'm t-tired," I manage, even as Z'hren hiccups and tugs on Vaza's long, gray-streaked hair. "I'm tired and my baby hates me."

Vaza reaches down and caresses my head as if I'm a child, and I lean against his big leg, utterly defeated. "He is just a kit, my beautiful one," he murmurs. "He will soon realize who loves him and who is always there to pick him up. Do not let it hurt your heart."

"Easy for you to say." I swipe at my eyes. "He doesn't hate the sight of you."

"Because I smell familiar and I look familiar. I am big and horned. You, my pretty one, are small and human he does not know what to think of that." Vaza tweaks my ear. "It will be all right, my heart. Be patient."

I know he's right. I know it. But my heart just hurts. I never thought of myself as a bad mama. Heck, if anything's defined me, it's loving and caring for others. Even when I didn't have a child at home, I still nurtured—coworkers, friends, anyone that crossed my path would be coddled by Mama Gail. Since landing here, I've held and comforted so many babies, pressing kisses to their faces and rocking them for hours on end while their mamas were busy. I love children.

I especially love Z'hren, but the feeling isn't mutual. "It's not fair," I manage, and then grimace in the darkness because I sound like I'm whining. Heck, I know I'm whining. I can't help it, though. I look up at Vaza and see through the faint glow of his eyes—and Z'hren's—that the baby's cuddled against him, relaxed as if Vaza has always been his father.

It's so unfair.

"He will come around," my man reassures me. "You told me before of your Cal-fin. Did he never fuss as a kit?"

"Calvin?" I snort through my tears, aching at the memory of my sweet boy and his smile. "Are you kidding? He was the crankiest child ever. There wasn't a bug going around that he wouldn't catch, and he would just get so damn angry at the world." I think of my baby boy from so many years ago, remembering the feel of him in my arms as if it were yesterday. "If it wasn't colic, it was an ear infection, or sinuses, or some other nonsense."

"And was he easily comforted?" Vaza asks, his hand caressing my cheek before he lifts it, and in the next moment I hear the low thump of his hand on the baby's back as Z'hren starts to fuss again.

"Easily comforted? My Calvin? Hell no." I shake my head, remembering. "The only thing that ever made him stop fussing when he felt bad was the boob. Sometimes he'd just nurse for hours, not really drinking but just needing the comfort..."

My words die away.

I blink.

I'm an idiot. "Oh my lord. Smack my head and call me a fool, Vaza." I jump to my feet, excited. Of course.

I'd forgotten all about nursing and skin to skin contact. I'd forgotten that nothing made Calvin settle quicker than putting him to my breast and letting him soothe himself to sleep with some suckling. Z'hren is mine, but I haven't been treating him like he's truly *mine*. There are no bottles here, and Z'hren's still young enough that I imagine he remembers what it's like to nurse.

"I...do not wish to do that?" Vaza says, clearly bewildered. "Why would I hit your head and call you names? I adore you—"

"It's an expression," I tell him quickly, and take the baby from his arms. "I've just been distracted, that's all. I know what he needs." And when Z'hren immediately starts to fuss, I open the front of my tunic, exposing one small breast, and slide him into nursing position.

I don't put him right up against my breast—I want to see if he reaches for me, or if I'm crazy. I don't have any milk, but maybe, just maybe, this'll be enough to comfort him.

My heart flips over in my chest when he immediately nuzzles against my skin, seeking out my nipple. He latches on a moment later and I can feel his tiny mouth working, trying to drink. New tears come to my eyes and I stroke his cheek as memories flood through my mind, of holding Calvin like this and just feeling so at peace with my baby at my breast.

Z'hren whimpers, tugging at my nipple in frustration when no milk comes out.

"Shh, little man," I murmur, gently stroking his hair. I suspect he's not really all that hungry. He just wants to be held. He wants comforting.

He wants his mama.

He latches on again, trying hard, and Vaza watches quietly, kneeling next to me. His hand brushes over my arm, as if he wants to be part of the circle. I smile at him, wanting to touch him but needing both hands to hold Z'hren, who's heavier than any human baby. Within a minute, maybe two, he settles down, his sucking slowing down and his breathing evening out. He's back to sleep, and my heart is full.

"He wants to nurse," I murmur to Vaza. "But I don't have any milk."

"Go to the healer in the morning," he tells me, all confidence. "She will be able to help."

"Are you sure?"

In the dim light, he shrugs. "What can it hurt to ask?"

He's got me there. "All right," I whisper. "I'll go at first light." I can't stop touching Z'hren, though. I run a fingertip along his little ear, the curve of his fat cheek, and he sleeps on, my nipple in his mouth.

"Do you want me to take him?" Vaza asks.

"Not just yet." I want to hold him all night and right on through morning. This is the first time I've been able to hold him in my arms and not have him scream in my face. I want to enjoy it for a little bit longer.

My man chuckles, but I think he understands. He caresses my arm again. "Do not hold him all night, then. I want my turn at your teats."

And I giggle like a schoolgirl, just because I'm so happy. So *relieved*.

6

GAIL

*T*he next morning, I gather Z'hren in my arms, bundle him up, and kiss Vaza goodbye. He's heading out this morning for more hunting, this time with two of the girls, and I give him a cheery smile and a playful swat on the ass. "Don't stay out too late."

Vaza gives me a speculative look. "Your mood is good, female."

"I feel good," I tell him, and I don't even mind that Z'hren's already fussing in my arms. He needs to eat, and he's squirming wildly. I suspect he's trying to slide into nursing position, but my tunic's not open and there's no food there yet, anyhow.

He leans in and caresses one of my nipples through my tunic. "Save some of that good feeling for when I return home later today."

I shiver, grinning. "Don't make promises you don't intend to keep, old man."

"Oh, I will keep them, my young beauty." And he winks at me, his hand sliding to caress my ass. "Put our son to sleep early, because his mother will be spending time in the furs with his father tonight."

I give another high-pitched giggle of happiness, sounding like a woman half my age. "You rogue. Go and teach those young women how to hunt before they start to wonder what's keeping you."

"They will know what's keeping me," he says, and pulls me into his arms, the baby sandwiched between us. He nibbles lightly on my ear, clearly frisky this morning. "They will say, 'That Vaza is claiming his pretty mate again this morning. What stamina he has!'"

I snort. "I can assure you no one is saying that, you big goof. I love you. Now go and do your thing and I'm going to go visit the healer and see if we can't get some milk started."

He kisses me, pinches my ass like the horny old dog that he is, and then heads out, weapons in hand. I watch him go, pleased, and sit down on the blankets to feed Z'hren one of his special bars. He gnaws on it for a moment and then fusses at me, as if displeased.

"Oh, I know. I want you to drink milk, too," I tell him, wiping his mouth clean of food as I smile at him. "But you and I are gonna have to be patient a little longer. All right?"

He stares up at me with those big baby eyes, so brilliantly blue with his khui...and then bellows his displeasure in my face.

Figures.

I keep smiling, though. Vaza's sweet morning flirtation did a lot to help my mood, and so did last night's suckling session. I'm positive Z'hren will stop hating me at some point, sooner if I can get my breasts to start producing milk. Plus, I can't help but feel that breast milk will be so much better for him than what he's been eating.

I'm just embarrassed I didn't think of it sooner.

I change his clothes after breakfast, wipe him down and sing silly songs to him as he sucks on one fist after another, as if giving them all a try before deciding one tastes the best. He starts to fuss again, and I scoop him up and decide to head off to find Veronica.

She's not by the fire, and neither is Angie. Of course not. Last night was a big feast that I didn't really enjoy because Z'hren was so miserable and Angie's water broke. I guess she had her baby. I clutch Z'hren tighter to me. If I can't nurse him...maybe Angie can alongside her baby? I hate the thought, but at the same time, I know my little man needs milk. I have to do what's best for him.

I head toward the fire, because Liz is there with her little ones. "Hey lady," I say to her, hefting Z'hren in my arms. "Which of these tents is Veronica and Ashtar's?"

She freezes while handing Aayla a bowl. Raashel just keeps on eating. "What's wrong?" Liz demands, her eyes wide as she looks at the crying baby in my arms. "Is Z'hren sick? Is he okay?"

"Everything is fine," I reassure her. "I just wanted to ask her something for me."

Liz relaxes, putting a hand to her brow and visibly deflating.

"You okay, Mommy?" Aayla asks.

"Yeah, Mommy just got a few more gray hairs," she says, patting her daughter's shoulder. "Eat your breakfast."

"Your hair is already gray and yellow," Raashel points out helpfully.

Liz just shakes her head, looking at me. "That's called blonde, baby." She looks at me and we share that moment of quiet mom amusement. "You want a daughter? I have a spare."

I chuckle. "Nah. Got my arms full with this one."

"They're up the hill," Liz tells me, reaching out and smoothing one of Raashel's little braids. "Last tent past the Tall Horn clan, just past R'jaal's dwelling. You can't miss it."

"Thanks," I tell her, racking my memory as to which one of the newcomers is R'jaal. My brain eventually reminds me that he's tall, lean, with enormous horns and a sharp, almost hungry expression on his face. He's the one that watches all the women like a starving man, I'd be willing to bet.

I head in the direction of the Tall Horn clan's tents. Shadowed Cat is in the caves, along with the unmated girls—a different set of caves, of course—and so the tents are clustered in a few different groups. Tall Horn is in the back of one of the twisty canyons, I'm guessing, and I take Z'hren on a walk down the beach, looking at each cluster of tents and trying to remember who is who.

I know I'm heading in the right direction when one of the tents at the far end of the canyon opens up, and a big, golden body steps out into the morning air, stretching. Naked. That'd be Ashtar, Veronica's mate. I stare at his package, just for a moment, because I'm old, not dead.

No spur. Huh. Vaza wins in that department. Once you get the spur, you don't settle for second best anymore.

Still thinking about spurs and my man, I hike up the beach towards Ashtar. "Hey there, is your mate awake?"

He scratches his bare chest with his big claws, oblivious to his nakedness or the fact that he's got morning wood. Lots of it. "Not yet. Why? Are you sick?" He looks more irritated than sympathetic.

"No, but I do have a favor to ask."

Ashtar looks sour at the thought. "Of course you do. Everyone is determined to have their share of my mate. She is wearing herself thin helping everyone."

"Well, mine was a pretty simple ask, but if it's gonna be a problem," I begin lightly.

A hand emerges from the tent and grabs Ashtar's ankle. "You be quiet, crankypants. I'm the healer. It's what I do." A moment later, Veronica peeks out of the tent, squinting up at me. Her hair's a messy nest of bedhead and post-sex tangles and she yawns. "You can ignore him. The doctor is in."

I eye Ashtar, but he only rolls his eyes and squats in front of the tent, which is real, real awkward for me as I get a bird's eye view of some serious dangling. "I only want to make sure you do not exhaust yourself, my mate," he says to Veronica. "The pregnant female had her kit last night—"

"Yes, and she hardly needed me, did she?" Veronica says pertly. "Thing practically slid right out of her." She waves me in again. "Besides, babe, this is Gail. You know she wouldn't ask if it wasn't important."

I hesitate, feeling guilty. Veronica has been stretching herself thin lately, but I hate to leave. I want this so badly, but I also don't want poor Veronica to wear herself out. "It's really no big deal. I can come back."

"Nonsense. Come sit down. I'm practically dressed. And Ashtar was just about to put some pants on."

"Was I?" The golden-skinned man rumbles with amusement. "I do not recall that."

"You know I don't like you parading the goods," she teases back. "Do it for my sanity."

He laughs, and when she holds out a fur wrap, he rolls his eyes good-naturedly and puts it on, tucking it at his waist. "Better?"

"Much. Gail?" She looks at me expectantly.

I consider it a moment more and then duck into the tent, Z'hren in my arms.

Inside, the air is several degrees warmer than the brisk morning, and there's a hint of sex in the air. That's normal, given that they just resonated, and after being a slave for a few years, nothing can shock me. I don't mind it. Just shows that they're happy and in love. Ain't nothing wrong with that. The tent's a bit of a mess, with furs everywhere and baskets of goods haphazardly cast about. Veronica tries to straighten up, yawning, and I take a seat on a pillow near the unlit fire pit. "Don't worry about cleaning up on my account. You're a busy woman."

She beams at me, thumps the pillow in her hand, and then immediately lies down on it. "Don't tell Ashtar, but I'm pretty sleepy," she admits with a yawn. "He worries."

"He's your man," I agree, trying to settle a squirming Z'hren in my arms. "He's allowed to worry about you." I think about what she said earlier. "Angie's baby...it's okay?"

"Oh, fat as a butterball and cute as a button."

"You called it a thing, though?" An awful thought occurs to me. "Is it...not human?"

Veronica just laughs. "Don't worry on that account. Thing, baby, whatever. I'm still figuring out this whole 'maternal' thing." And she pats her stomach. "Sorry, dragon-baby. You're gonna be a 'thing' to me too, no matter how cute you are."

It reminds me just how young all these girls are. Veronica could be my daughter. Hell, all of them could be. "Is she happy, at least?"

"Ecstatic," Veronica agrees. "It's a gorgeous baby. I won't spoil any more about it because that's hers to share, but it really is beautiful and healthy."

I smile. "That's all that matters."

Z'hren looks up at me, screws his little face up, and wails.

"Speaking of," I say, adjusting him in my arms. I decide that there's no point in hiding anything or pretending, so I open the front of my tunic and set Z'hren against my breast. He immediately latches on, nursing, and then lets out a whimper of frustration when there's nothing. "Can you make me lactate?" I ask. "Because I want to be able to feed my baby."

She blinks at me, surprised, and then a slow smile curves her mouth. "I bet I can."

7

GAIL

A short time later, I leave Veronica and Ashtar's tent, my breasts throbbing from her ministrations.

All she did was touch my hand and chitchat, but I feel…different. My boobs feel heavier and my body hums from within with a burst of energy.

I'm full of hope, too, that we might have this thing figured out.

"You're already on the right track," she told me as she held my hand. "I can feel your body's gearing up to produce milk. Maybe because you've done it in the past and you're nursing him now? Whatever it is, I just need to give it a little nudge. It'll probably be good for you to massage your breasts on the regular until it comes in, as weird as that sounds. And come back in a few days if nothing's happening, and we'll give your body another nudge."

I thanked her, making a mental note to create a small gift of some kind for her. Ashtar's right, we do take her for granted, and she works hard to keep everyone in the tribe healthy.

She touched Z'hren next and frowned a little to herself. "Whatever he's been eating has been giving him an upset tummy. I can feel it hurting and bloated. I'll work on that, too."

I felt like the worst mama ever. "I didn't know. He's been so fussy lately that it's been hard to tell."

"The diet on the island was pretty different, I imagine." She patted my arm. "You're doing the best you can, like all of us."

Her words make me feel a little better. At least she's able to help him, and I can give him that much. I thank her once more and joke that she can go back to doting on Ashtar. Veronica just shakes her head with a smile. Her 'schedule' is busy, because now that she's done with Z'hren, she's heading over to visit T'chai (who I haven't met) and his mate, and then stopping by Angie's cave. I feel guilty for taking up her time, but it's clear Veronica enjoys being needed.

So I take my sleepy son home and nap, remembering to squeeze my breasts to try and bring the milk in faster.

A warm hand caresses my shoulder, waking me from sleep. With a groan, I roll over and rub my eyes, looking up into Vaza's handsome, weathered face. "You're back already?"

"The one called Pen-ee twisted her ankle," he says, shrugging. "It seemed wise to return home before the day was too long. She can go see the healer and I can slide under the furs with my mate." Vaza grins at me, pulling the furs back and eyeing my mostly naked body with obvious pleasure. "It is clear I made a good decision to come back. You look lonely."

I chuckle. "Do I, now?"

"Very," he says solemnly. "Lonely and cold. It is my duty as your mate to warm your fragile human body."

"Fragile nothing," I tell him, amused. "You are treading on thin ground, my man." But I lift the furs up so he can slide in next to me. "Z'hren?"

"Sleeping."

"He'll be awake soon," I tell him, and then cup my heavy-feeling breasts. "I went to see the healer this morning."

"And?" His gaze slides to my hands, because he's a man. He leans over and starts to unlace one of his boots.

"She thinks I can start producing milk in a few days. I'm supposed to play with my breasts to encourage things along." And I give them a teasing squeeze, casting a sexy smile in his direction. "Such a chore, right?"

"Not a chore at all," he tells me, and relaces his boot.

I sit up on my elbows. "What are you doing?"

"I am going to let Lo-ren watch Z'hren for a time so I can spend my afternoon helping my mate's milk come in." He gives me a heated look. "This will require all of our concentration." He pauses and then adds, "And Lo-ren offered to take him when I returned to camp."

I grin. Seems like we're going to get to have a lazy afternoon to ourselves. I like the thought. It's been days and days since we had any alone time and I didn't realize how much I missed it. I wouldn't trade Z'hren for the world, but if Lauren wants to take him regularly for an afternoon, I won't complain. "Sounds good to me. Just tell her to avoid giving him the fatty bars she's been making. Something in them upsets his stomach." I bite my lip. "Does that sound accusing? I didn't even know it was a problem until I saw Veronica this morning and she said that was why he was fussing as much as he was. Should I get dressed and go with you to explain?" I sit up, about to get to my feet.

"You lie back and think of your mate and squeeze your teats," he tells me, a hand on my shoulder. "I will take our kit to Lo-ren and explain. If the healer said it, it must be true. Remain where you are." He turns away, then pauses and looks back at me. "And keep touching yourself."

"Yes, sir," I murmur, more than a little aroused at how decisive he is. Nothing sexier than a man that knows what he wants.

He returns within a matter of minutes, the basket gone. His bright, glowing eyes are full of heat as he carefully closes the tent behind us and slides the bone latch into the loop, indicating that we want privacy. It takes everything I have not to wiggle with excitement as he stalks forward a few steps, then looms over the furs. "Have you been working your breasts like you should, my beautiful human mate?"

"Of course," I tell him, and shift so the blanket falls back and he can see me kneading and squeezing my small tits as if they're something spectacular. They ache, the tips ultra-sensitive, but I take that as a good sign and keep going. I can stand a little bit of pain if it means my baby gets to nurse that much quicker.

"You are a very well-behaved female today," he murmurs, stripping his cloak off and tossing it to the ground. "This is very different from my mouthy Shail."

"Mmm," I agree, grinning. "I've been a good girl all afternoon."

"You must want something." He slides his hand up and down the front of his loincloth suggestively, and I fight the urge to giggle like a schoolgirl.

"A bit of spur, perhaps?" I keep my tone light, even as I let my fingertips trail over my dark nipples, circling them. I love "play-ing" with Vaza. After dating men who took sex—and life—so very seriously, I love that he's got a frisky side to him and loves when I tease him right back. I could play Naughty Nurse with him and he'd eat it up. Or Naughty Student. Heck, I could even be a Naughty Rabbit and he'd have no clue what was going on, but he'd be down for it. He just wants to be with me, and that's the biggest aphrodisiac of all—a man that practically worships the ground I walk upon.

"You get the spur when I know you have done a good job on your teats, female," he tells me, his voice playfully stern. "Not a moment sooner."

"Oh, but my hands are SO tired," I mock-complain, circling my hard nipples with two fingertips. "If only there was someone who could help me out."

Vaza groans, and he practically flings his loincloth across the tent. Now he's in nothing but his boots, and his eyes are blue fire as he drops to his knees. "Do you need assistance, then?" He practically pants the words out, and I can see the hard, ridged length of him jutting from his corded thighs. Oooh, yum. This man is a treat.

"I bet you could do a fantastic job," I practically purr at him, arching my back.

"Allow me," he says, as if I'm doing him a favor, and then he slides into the furs next to me, his hard blue body warm against mine. One hand reverently cups my breast even as his face lowers to the other. A moment later, he takes my nipple into his mouth and sucks hard.

I gasp, shocked at how sensitive my breasts are. Just that small, not-unexpected touch sends a bullet of sensation through me. He groans at my response, sliding his hand from my other breast to the one his mouth is latched onto. He squeezes it, feeding more of it into his hungry mouth, and continues to suck hard.

I grab his hair, writhing against his mouth. "Oh, that's good, Vaza. That's really good."

He lifts his head long enough to drag his tongue over my aching nipple in a slow lick. "It does not hurt?"

"Never. Just keep going." I'm super sensitive, but it's not painful. I just feel as if I might come apart if he toys with them long enough. Already I can feel my pussy's ultra-slick with arousal, which is nice. Sometimes it takes me a while to get wet, but not today. And when he lightly scrapes his teeth over my nipple, I cry out, pulling on his thick, gray-streaked hair. "You are a devil," I tell him as I press my breast up to his mouth for more attention. "A big, sexy devil. My devil."

Vaza groans, and his hand slides from my breast down to between my legs. I can hear his grunt of approval when he finds that I'm already sopping wet. He shifts his body and his big cock rubs up against my thigh even as he continues to work my breast, nipping and sucking at the small mound and the erect tip.

It feels like he spends eternity on my breasts. He cups my mound, but his hand remains on the curls there, a silent tease as he switches from my left breast to my right and gives it the same intense loving that the other received. By the time he lifts his head again, I'm squirming like a wild woman under him, panting demands for him to touch my pussy, to find my clit and touch it like he's touching my breasts. I need him all over me. I need his mouth and his hands and his everything—especially his spur.

"Gimme your spur," I demand when I can take it no longer. I push my thighs wide apart and slide my hand over his, pressing his big fingers against my aching, wet folds. I rub his fingers over my slick heat and nearly come apart at that, especially when he chuckles. "You're such a damn tease, Vaza."

"Beg me," he says, his eyes hot as he leans in and nips at the tip of one breast once more.

Oooh, we're playing that game, are we? "Beg you?" I shiver at how dominant he can get at times. I thought I'd hate a man that got all bossy on me, but in bed? In bed, I'm all over it. It's just another game, and a fun one. "I'm not going to beg you, you naughty man."

"Then I shall keep tormenting you," Vaza says, his breath hot on my stomach, and I shiver all over again as the tip of his tail flicks along the inside of my thigh. "You are mine, my beautiful human, and I will not give you what you need until you realize it."

"Maybe you should beg me," I manage between panting, even as his mouth dips lower and he brushes his lips against the curls on my mound. "Beg me so you can take this hot, tight pussy."

He chuckles. "I could take it now and you would thank me," he murmurs, giving my folds a teasing hint of a lick. Just a hint. His hands tighten on my thighs. "I would push inside you and you would say, 'Oh Vaza, fill me with your enormous blue cock. Make my cunt shiver on your rod. I am but a weak human female and need to come so hard."

I want to giggle at his ridiculousness, but then he sucks on my clit and I lock my thighs tight around his shoulders, pinning him in place. "Oh fuck me, right there, baby."

He grunts his pleasure at the taste of me, and then there are no sounds in the tent other than my soft cries and the sound of his wet, thorough licking and sucking. He gives my clit the same attention he gave my breasts, and I come so damn hard, my thighs quaking against his shoulders.

"My beauty," he murmurs as he wrings spasm after spasm of plea-sure from my body. "My heart. My lovely Shail. Never have I seen anything as perfect as you. You fill my spirit with a fever I cannot quench—nor do I want to. I want you like this under me, forever."

And that's another thing I love about this man—he can go from playful horndog to sexy poet in a matter of moments. "Vaza," I breathe, reaching for him. "I want you. Come take your mate."

He shifts his big body—so impossibly big compared to my smaller frame, but he's always so gentle with me. A moment after his large form covers mine, he slicks his cock up and down my soaking folds, wetting his length with my juices. Then he pushes inside me, and it feels so good that my groan is louder than his.

"Shall I give you more, my star? My morning sunlight?"

"Give me everything you've got," I demand of him, and he does. Vaza fucks me, fast and hard and oh-so-deliciously. It doesn't take long for me to come again—not with the spur shuttling against my clit with every stroke of his cock into me. Once I come again, the full-body shudder tells him that now it's his turn, and it's not more than a breath or two before he groans my name with his own release. He rocks into me slowly, whispering all kinds of platitudes and calling me beautiful things. His snow flower. His perfect sunrise. His treasure. It would all be slightly ridiculous if he wasn't so damn sincere, and as it is, it's just sweet. I slip my arms around his neck as he collapses into the furs next to me and watch him recover, because looking at him's a treat.

"This is nice," I tell him, sliding my hand over his plated pectorals. "Real nice."

"I am glad I returned early," he agrees, sweaty and pleased. "Pen-ee needs to injure herself more often."

"Not a nice thing to wish," I say with a laugh.

"Not a bad injury," he tells me, because he doesn't have a single mean bone in his body. "Just one that will allow me to forget my duties for an afternoon and tuck my mate under the furs with me." He pulls me tight against him and kneads one breast, teasing the nipple into a hard peak once more. "Your teats—how are they?"

"Sensitive," I admit.

"They feel larger," he agrees. "Heavy. I like your teats as small, perfect little nuggets, but I like them like this, too."

"I'm not sure I like my body being referred to as 'nuggets,'" I say, amused. "Exactly what kind of nuggets are we talking about?"

"Big, meaty nuggets," he immediately amends, a wicked smile on his face. "Is that not what I said?"

"Not exactly."

"Your hearing is going with your old age." Vaza manages to keep a straight face. "It is a good thing I am here to interpret for you."

"Boy, you did not just call me flat chested AND old." But I'm smiling because he is, too, and I know he loves the way I look. He hasn't been able to take his eyes off me since the day we met. I glance down at my boobs. "You think they're a little bigger? Really?"

He nods. "I could tell when I put your teat into my mouth. If they are sensitive, do they need more rubbing?" He caresses one with a big hand and gives me an encouraging look.

Even on Earth I never met a man with as much stamina as Vaza. I chuckle. "Give me a moment to catch my breath, and then I'll let you play with my 'nuggets' all you like." I glance toward the tent flaps and then hesitate. "How long should we leave Z'hren with Lauren, do you think?"

"All afternoon," he tells me promptly, and pulls me down against him so he can lick my nipple once more.

So much for catching my breath. I bite back a gasp as he begins to tease it expertly, and try to remain focused. "I don't want to impose—"

"Shail, my beautiful one, let Lo-ren take him for a time." He nuzzles my breast and then glances up. "Do not forget that you are Shail as well as Z'hren's mother. You can be both without letting one take over the other."

He's got a point. After Calvin died, I wrapped myself up in my grief as my identity and didn't care about the rest of the world. Maybe if Shaun would have helped me cope instead of shutting me out, it would have been different. But Vaza's an entirely different sort of partner, and I know he won't let me sink into mommy mode without forgetting Gail. He's supportive and loving—there's no doubt about that—but he's also firm with boundaries. "You're a good man, you know that?"

Vaza looks smug. "You always say that after I give you spur."

I push against his shoulder, nudging him onto his back. "You always remember that I'm Gail first, though, and I love that. You never try to make me be anything other than I am."

"Because you have my heart," he says simply, touching my short, natural curls and studying my face. "I find everything about you perfect. Why would I change any of it? It is Shail that I adore. I want all of Shail, not pieces of someone else."

He always knows the right thing to say. With a sultry little smile, I sit up, deciding that compliments can be rewarded. "Now, let me show you one of Gail's tricks..."

And as I straddle him, his eyes light up.

8

GAIL

We make love for hours, and it's nice to spend a leisurely afternoon between the furs like a pair of teenagers. Once my stomach rumbles, though, Vaza is back into protector mode. He stokes our small fire, melts fresh water so I can wash up, and then disappears out to grab us portions of whatever the camp food is tonight. With so many hunters practicing, there's always plenty of fresh game and so I'm not surprised when Vaza returns with an entire dvisti haunch. It's raw, of course. I still haven't gotten used to raw, cold meat for dinner, but I tolerate it because it's Vaza's favorite and the scent of cooking meat tickles his nose unpleasantly.

As Vaza cuts our dinner up, Lauren and K'thar stop by with Z'hren. We invite them to share our food, since there's plenty of it, and I'm pleased when they accept. I love company, and I know Vaza does, too.

Z'hren immediately reaches for me when Lauren approaches,

and my heart swells. Maybe he missed me. I hold my arms out and he flings himself into my grasp, and then immediately burrows into my tunic, looking to latch on.

I turn discreetly away from the others because I'm not sure how Lauren and K'thar will react, and open my tunic. He makes a few happy little grunts, quickly followed by frustrated sounds when nothing comes out.

"He...ate not too long ago," Lauren says, her voice soft. "I didn't realize he was still hungry."

I adjust my tunic so the leather folds cover most everything, and then turn around to face them once more, resting a hand on Vaza's shoulder as I sit next to the fire. "I don't know if he is or not, but I think he just likes to suck. There's nothing there yet, anyhow. Veronica says it should take a few days."

Lauren rubs her ear and looks slightly embarrassed. "I never even thought of nursing. I feel bad, because I can't imagine eggs are any better for him."

"It took me a few days to come to it myself. It happens." I smile at her. "I think all of you did a fantastic job with him considering both his mother and father died."

"Well, you look really at home," Lauren says, hugging her knees. "Like you've done this before."

"I had a son once, back on Earth." When her look turns stricken, I shake my head. "I didn't leave him behind. He passed away some time ago."

"Oh, I'm so sorry." Lauren reaches for K'thar's hand, linking her fingers with his and glancing at her quiet mate.

The ache is old, and somewhat lessened by the sweet face buried in my tunic right now. Once, I might have spent the entire evening talking about Calvin, but that's part of my past, like everyone else here has a past. I think of all that Vaza's lost, and how he doesn't let it define him. He carries it with him, but it doesn't rule him day to day. He looks to the future with hope, and I'm learning to do the same. "It's all right," I say, and cast a smile in Vaza's direction. "Just means I don't have to worry about resonance messing with the good thing I've got going."

"There is nothing wrong with choosing what your heart wants," Vaza declares, and reaches out to brush his knuckles over my cheek in a caress.

"Nothing at all," I agree, then gesture at the food, waiting to be devoured. "Now, shall we eat? We've got an entire haunch of dvisti, ready to share."

THE NEXT MORNING, the sound of a baby crying rouses me from my sleep.

Z'hren.

I drag myself out of bed, groaning, because all of my limbs feel heavy and tired. Last night was a good night, if a late one. K'thar and Lauren sat around, drinking tea and sharing stories after dinner. A short time later, J'shel and N'dek joined us, and then our tent was full of people, nibbling on leftovers, laughing, and talking. It felt good. It felt like a family, and we loved the company. Z'hren went from lap to lap for a bit, and then settled down against my breast and went to sleep. It was very late when Vaza chased the last of them out, frowning at N'dek as he was piggybacked away by J'shel.

"That one has to learn to take care of himself again," my mate said.

"Give him time," I replied sleepily. "They said his wound was new." I can only imagine the grieving process for a missing limb. "He'll get back to himself soon enough, whatever the old 'himself' was."

Vaza just grunts. I know it's hard for him to understand sitting around idly. He's told me that after his mate died—and later when his son did—he threw himself into hunting and working hard around the cave so he wouldn't have to spend much time alone at his fire. Everyone goes through it differently, though, and I make a mental note to be supportive of N'dek and see if there's anything I can help him with.

He's young, after all—they all are—and the mama in me can't let a child be miserable.

Which is why I crawl out of bed. I move to Z'hren's basket, clucking at him as he cries. "At some point, little man, you're going to wake up happy and not screaming," I tell him softly.

Today is not that day, though. He blasts my face with another angry demand, legs and arms thrashing. His angry cries fill the tent, and when I lean over to pick him up, I notice that my soft, brushed leather tunic is sticking to my front as if it's wet.

Startled, I pause and undo the loose ties that angle artfully down the side, until my tunic is open. Z'hren screams louder, wanting to be picked up, and as he does, I see milk beading on my nipples. I touch one breast, surprised, and find that it's heavier than it felt yesterday, and tender. Even as I touch it, more milk dribbles out.

I don't know if I want to cry with relief or scream with joy.

Z'hren is doing plenty of screaming on his own, though, and I'm practically weeping with happiness as I pick him up. "Hey, hey," I shush, giddy. "Come here, baby boy. Come here."

He reaches for me as I pick him up, his cries immediately dying to an unhappy whimper, and I settle him against my breast. He grunts, making greedy little sounds as he latches on and begins to pull. For the first time, there's milk for him, and he sucks harder, as if he's been starving all this time. Milk bubbles at the corners of his little mouth and trickles down his chin, but he doesn't stop drinking.

And my heart is full. Happy tears fall down my cheeks, and I gaze down at my baby with love. My son. My Z'hren. One small hand curls against my breast, and then the other, and he opens his eyes and watches my face as he nurses, and my silly heart melts just a little more with every passing second.

"There you go, little man," I whisper. "Mama's got you."

"Mama is sad?" a familiar, sexy voice murmurs in my ear. A warm finger brushes my cheek, and Vaza leans over my shoulder, nuzzling at my skin. "Or are these happy tears?"

"Good morning, love. And they are most definitely happy tears." I beam at him, then down at our child. "Look at how perfect our son is."

"He looks just like you," Vaza teases, and I giggle as if that's the funniest thing I've ever heard. "Look at him," he urges again.

I do, and I'm shocked to see that Z'hren's blended his camouflage to match my dark skin. My heart aches with wonder at the sight. I knew he could camouflage just like the others in his tribe, but I never expected this...

The suction breaks on my nipple, and I see Z'hren watching me. His little face breaks into a smile, his mouth covered in milk, but it's a smile and it's for me.

I smile back.

AUTHOR'S NOTE

Hello again!

I hope you enjoyed Gail's (long-awaited) story. I always feel a tiny bit guilty when I release a novella instead of a full-length novel, because I know you guys anticipate every story with so much enthusiasm. And I know how it feels to get into a story and want it to never, never end. In my head, though, Gail's story has always been a novella. Not because she's less interesting than everyone else, but because she's at a different point in her life. In your twenties, everything is a Big. Deal. and by the time you get older, you get tired of that shit. You know who you are and you're confident in yourself. I could have artificially added some conflict just to draw the story out, but I hate stories where happy couples are angry at each other throughout the entire book. I just hate it! And I don't want to do that to my characters.

So what you get is a sweet slice of life about babies and older people having a fantastic time in the sack together. It is what it is. ;)

I know some readers were super excited at the thought of Gail resonating, but doing so would break a lot of rules I've set up for the world already. Vaza is a widower, and the khui picks one mate and one mate alone. I would have to give him a new khui (which is extremely rare) and then it would have to pick Gail. As for Gail, her reproductive organs would basically have to start up again, and I hesitate (mentally) to do something like that for a lot of reasons. There's absolutely nothing wrong with being older and being done with having babies. There is absolutely nothing wrong with adoption, either. I feel like it's a loving, wonderful alternative. There's also nothing wrong with having zero babies at all...but when I created Gail, I made her a maternal mama hen to all the lost chicks, so it made perfect sense for her to adopt instead of magicking so much stuff to make Vaza and Gail resonate. I know you're thinking to yourself, Ruby, it's fucking FICTION, do what you want!

Yes, it is. But in my head, there are rules, and the rules must be obeyed.

Also, Gail and Vaza are perfectly happy where they are. And so is Z'hren. At any rate, for those of you rooting for Gail's Uterus Rebirth, I'm sorry!

You guys might also be wondering why this is in Icehome instead of Ice Planet Barbarians, series-wise. I thought it slid in perfectly between book 3 and the upcoming book 5 of Icehome, whereas I feel like Ice Planet Barbarians is at a different place in its timeline (but not done!) – so Icehome it is. I hope it's not too confusing.

As for what is next, my goal is to write Icehome #5 next (let's be honest, I'm already knee-deep in it). It's tentatively called ANGIE'S GLADIATOR and will NOT be ménage. Angie gets one man, and the other's going to have to figure out what to do with himself when he's no longer part of a team. I've been asked to make it ménage, and I've also been asked NOT to make it ménage, but the plan has always been to give Angie just one man.

I'm fascinated by what a 'twin' (or okay, clone) does and thinks when one twin finds his happy ever after and the other does not... at least, not right away. To me, that's a way more fun storyline than throwing both hot sauce and ketchup into Angie's sandwich. ;)

After ANGIE'S GLADIATOR I'm going to switch back to Fire-blood Dragons and hopefully will have Liam and Andrea's story out just after the new year. I'm already excited to write it and have been daydreaming out scenes in my head, a sure sign that the story's ready to spill itself out onto the page.

Thank you, once again, for being such amazing fans. <3

Ruby

PS - In the Print Edition, I've included a free Christmas story that I posted on Facebook - enjoy!

A GIFT FOR DRENOL

DRENOL

It is hard to be old in a tribe full of young ones. I watch the tribe move about the village, racing about as if they do not have hand after hand of years ahead of them. There are females everywhere, their kits darting back and forth across the cobbled stone walkways that make paths through the new village.

Bah. New village. I prefer the caves of my youth. They were much warmer than these little huts, and the worn, smooth floors were easier on the feet than the cobblestones. But times change, and tribes change. Hektar is no longer chief, but his son Vektal. And Vektal has a human mate, a pale, stringy-looking creature with no nose to speak of and a bushy, curly mane. She has a nice smile, at least, and has bred him two strong daughters and carries a third kit. He seems happy enough.

They all do, actually. Now more than ever, the tribe is full of happiness. It does not matter that it is the brutal season and the winds roar overhead, carrying blankets of thick snow to cover the landscape. Here in this canyon, we are protected, and so everyone wanders about, smiling like fools. Even Haeden, who has always been reasonable and quiet in the past, has an idiot smile on his face as his little mate chatters and chatters, rubbing her rounded belly and they string up colorful seeds along the walls of their hut.

Jo-see. Bah. That one is determined to repopulate the entire tribe with her womb alone.

I snort, amused at my own joke.

Everywhere I look, I see families moving around the village. They dart from hut to hut, decorating with banners and boughs, seed chains and tiny basketed trees that Salukh's mate brought out from the long-house. The base of each tree is covered with a red-dyed leather covering to protect the roots, and the tree branches themselves are covered in strange ornaments. Each one has been placed in front of the entrance of a hut, and the kits are so excited at the sight of each one that they scream and laugh, racing around like crazed metlaks.

My bones ache just looking at them.

Drayan moves out of our hut and to my side, stretching. "They enjoy this No-Poison thing, the kits."

I grunt.

"I like that they decorate the huts," Drayan continues, oblivious to my surly mood. He crosses his arms over his chest, his snow-white braids stark against his skin. "You know who would have liked this?"

I stiffen, my eyes narrowing.

"Koloi."

"My mate would not have approved of this nonsense," I grumble at him. "She was sensible."

"She painted everything she could get her hands on, you old fool." Drayan just grins at me, as if bringing up my mate will make me pleasant. He should know better.

I just scowl at him. Some of us age cheerfully, like Drayan, who greets every day with a smile and does not mind that he sometimes has to walk with a cane to support his weight. Some age into fools, like Vaza, who went to the other village with his female. And Vadren, who loses his wits a little more every day.

Me, I aged into an old, bitter hunter. My mate, my sweet Koloi, is long gone. There are no grown kits to look after, no family at my fire. Our son died not many turns after he was born and there was never another. Such is life. If it has made me unpleasant to be around, I care not. Fools like Drayan will always try to talk to me. Koloi's sister Kemli tries to include me when she gathers her family to her hearth, but she has all of her kits alive and grown, with families of their own. Even now, she is cooking a mountain of food for her son Zennek and his mate, and the mates of Pashov and Salukh. Her hearth is full of human females and their kits, and I do not want to spend my time there. I know if I stay here, she will bring me food and that is all I need.

Stupid No-Poison haul-day.

As if he can read my thoughts, Drayan gives my shoulder a thump. "Are you going to Kemli's fire this night?"

"Why?" I frown up at him. "So the humans can talk my horns off?"

"Jo-see will not be there," he teases, knowing my particular dislike for that one and her chattering mouth. "Stay-see and Teef-nee are not noisy like her. And Mar-len is amusing."

I just roll my eyes.

"You should spend the evening with them," he encourages. "I will be going to Meh-gann's fire. She is cooking for myself and Suh-mer and Warrek. It will be nice. And Vadren has been invited to Air-ee-yon-uh's fire since her mate is gone and she wants to cook for someone. If you do not want to go with Kemli's family, go and visit her?"

"No."

He gets a sly look on his face. "I bet if I tell Jo-see that you are eating alone she will come and insist on you spending the evening at their fire. Humans love this haul-day."

I glare at him and get to my feet. Or try to, but it's a struggle. My old bones do not respond like they used to. I manage to get up, and then I straighten to my full height and glare at him. "I am going to Kemli's, if only to shut you up."

Drayan laughs, pleased. "You will enjoy yourself, friend."

I somehow doubt that very much.

I arrive at Kemli's hut as late as possible. Even before I walk in, I can smell delicious scents...and I hear the murmur of voices. The hide she keeps over the door is pushed aside, welcoming any to walk in, and so I do and sit down by the fire immediately.

"Brother," Kemli says warmly, smiling at me. She is still lovely despite her age, and I imagine my Koloi might have looked like her if she would have lived longer. It makes my heart ache, but I manage to nod at her. "I am glad you are here. Are you hungry?"

"No," I say stubbornly. "I am only here because Drayan would not be quiet. I would rather be at home, where it is quiet." And I glare at the kits playing on the floor nearby.

Kemli only rolls her eyes and tweaks one of my braids. "I will get you a cup of tea anyhow. The food is not quite ready yet, is it, Stay-see?"

"Soon," the human woman says. That one is Pashov's mate, her son holding a bowl for her as she ladles a sweet-smelling mixture onto her flat metal baking tray. Nearby, Teef-nee's boy plays with Mar-len's daughter, a set of carved bone figures in front of them. Mar-len holds Stay-see's newest kit in her arms as she talks to her mate, and Teef-nee fiddles with something in her hands as she talks to Borran. It is crowded and hot in the hut, and I do not like it.

Kemli returns to my side and gives me a cup of tea. "Here, your favorite."

"I do not know how I am supposed to drink it when I am already melting," I tell her, scowling, but I take the tea anyhow.

She just pats my shoulder and moves back to the fire, stirring something before moving past Stay-see.

I notice Teef-nee's son watching me, and I frown in his direction. My backside aches from sitting on this rock, and I can already tell this will be a long evening. I bite back a sigh of irritation when the boy gets up, a carved figure clutched in his hand, and comes to my side. His eyes are wide and curious. He has the same mane that his mother does, the wild, tight curls that spin out like a cloud around his head and horns, but his skin is the same shade as his father's. He tilts his head at me, ignoring my scowl. "Do you want to play hunters with me and Zalene?"

And he holds out a carved figure to me. I take it from him, studying it. The carving is a dvisti. "Who did this?"

"Aehako."

I grunt. "He needs practice. His animals are not very good." I hand it back. "No, I do not want to play."

Lukti's mouth purses, unhappy. "Why are you mad?"

Am I to get no relief this day? "I am mad because I have to be here." I gesture at the too-crowded room, where there is barely room to breathe. "It is crowded. It is noisy. People want to feed me when I just want to be left alone. And my backside hurts because these seats are uncomfortable." I glare the last part at Kemli, who ignores me, a smile on her face.

"But it's a holiday," Lukti says, confused. "Everyone gets together with family on the holiday."

"Bah. Haul-day." I wave a hand in the air. "So you can put up ugly decorations? My mate could make a hut like this pretty. Koloi could paint better than any of these fools."

Instead of being offended, he looks interested. "Koloi? I haven't met her. Is she visiting Icehome like Pacy's Papa?"

His innocent words cut deep. "No."

He gets even more excited. "Is there a story about her?"

I wave a hand irritably, trying to shoo him away. "Leave me alone. My bones ache."

"Will you tell me a story next time? I love hearing stories." He is persistent, this one.

"I do not like you," I tell him, scowling. "Go away!"

Kemli is there a moment later, ushering the kit back to his mother. "Come, Lukti. Stay-see's cakes are almost done and you get the first one."

I grunt, pleased that she is taking him away. Far too many kits in this village, I decide. Far too many.

This haul-day cannot end quick enough.

LUKTI

After spending the evening at Nana Kemli's hut, me and Mommy walk back to our hut in the dark. I want to ask Mommy a bunch of questions, but she's real quiet, like she is when she's thinking about her spindle, so I'm quiet too. I know it makes her cry sometimes and I don't want to make her cry.

We go into our hut and our fire is nothing but coals, the inside chilly. "I'll make a fire, Mommy," I tell her.

"No, baby," she says absently. "It's bedtime. You know what that means."

It means that we do our No-Poison presents in the morning. I'm excited about that, but I know it won't be the same without Papa here. Mommy says he's being a good man and helping others that can't feed themselves and so we have to be strong, but sometimes I cry baby tears and wish he was home because I miss him. I think Mommy misses him, too. She's sad a lot of the time and so that's why she's always playing with her spindle. She told me once that if she got it to work, it'd almost be worth Papa being gone.

I take my boots off and set them in their drying spot, and then change into my sleep-tunic with its soft fur and the long "cape" in the back that Mommy made so I can tuck my feet into it on colder nights. I get under the blankets and wait for my kiss and my lullaby, but Mommy doesn't come over right away. She looks distracted, toying with her spindle by the faint light of the coals. I watch her tease the clump of Chompy's hair on it over and over again, but she gets frustrated and tosses it aside...and then picks it up again, frowning at it.

Maybe she won't mind if I ask... "Mommy?"

"Yes, baby?"

"Can I play ball with Holvek in the morning? After we share No-Poison gifts?" Normally I play ball with Papa in the morning on No-Poison day, but Papa isn't here.

"Sure, baby."

"I have to play ball with Holvek because Raashel's gone with her mommy and papa to Icehome."

"Mmm." She fusses with the spindle.

"Raashel's my bestest friend, but she's gone, so I guess Holvek can be my bestest friend now. He's not as good with the ball."

"Maybe if you play with him more, he'll get better," Mommy says, glancing over at me.

Oh, that's a good idea. Pleased, I settle back in the blankets and think about Papa over at Icehome camp. I hope someone made him a good No-Poison dinner tonight like Nana Kemli made for us. Then I think about old Drenol and how mean he was. He didn't like my toys and scowled at us kids all through dinner.

"Mommy?"

"Hmm?"

"How come Drenol's so mean? Nana Kemli always invites him to No-Poison dinner and he's always mad at everyone."

She moves over to my bed and sits down next to me, curling her legs under her. I sit up, because I love it when Mommy comes and hangs out in my bed. We sit together like we're sharing secrets and it makes me feel so special. "Was he mean to you, baby?" She touches a tuft of my mane, toying with it. Her spindle is in her lap, forgotten.

"Not to me. But he was mean to Nana Kemli and she was trying to be nice."

Mommy smiles, her teeth bright in the dark. "He's sad, baby. He's an old man and he doesn't have anyone left."

I scrunch my face up in a frown. Not have anyone left? But there are people everywhere, every day. "He has the tribe. He has all of us."

"But it's not the same. Remember when Raashel left and you were sad?" She squeezes my hand. "You're going to play ball with Holvek tomorrow instead of Papa or Raashel. You still have the tribe, but it's not the same, is it?"

It's not. I miss Papa so much, and Holvek is a good friend, but Raashel was different. She was smart and funny and always saying interesting things. Holvek just likes to wrestle and get dirty.

Maybe Drenol is missing his bestest friends too.

I sniff and wipe my hand across my nose. Thinking about sad things makes me sad and my eyes water.

"Oh, don't cry, baby. It's okay." Mommy's fingers brush over my face, and I immediately feel better.

"I don't like that Drenol doesn't have his friends. Should I ask him to play ball in the morning instead of Holvek?"

Mommy laughs softly. "He might be too old for that, baby."

"He did say his butt hurt when we were at Nana Kemli's." Butts must hurt when you get old.

Mommy just touches my cheek. "No ball for him. But I bet he'd like it if you'd go and talk to him for a while. Keep him company."

I wrinkle my nose. I don't want to spend more time with him. He didn't like my toys. "But he's mean, Mommy."

"Only because he's unhappy." She tweaks my ear. "Remember when Elly first got here?"

"She was smelly," I agree.

"Because she was scared and lonely. And she never talked to anyone, did she?" When I shake my head, Mommy continues. "It took time for her to be comfortable. Sometimes we do things when we're afraid because we're worried we're going to get hurt again. It takes time for us to relax and realize that people are nice just because they're nice. Give it time. I bet he could use a friend."

I think of Drenol. His face was covered in lines and his braids were snow white. Nana Kemli says that she has a gray hair for every story. Drenol must have *a lot* of stories...and I love stories.

"I'll try, Mommy."

She pulls me into her lap and cuddles me, and it's the best. Mommy cuddles make everything better.

Mommy and I share presents in the morning for No-Poison, and then I go out and play ball with Holvek for a little while. He has a new tunic from his mommy and big, padded gloves that his mommy called bahk-sing gloves. They're so you can hit each other as a game and it won't hurt. It's fun for a little bit, but Holvek wants to keep playing after I'm tired. He runs off to find Talie because she's strong, and I go inside. Mommy's still playing with her spindle, twirling it like a top. Her expression is excited, like it's doing something cool, and I slip back out again so I don't bother her.

I think about what Mommy said last night.

Mommy was right. It was a good holiday, but it isn't the same because Papa and Raashel aren't here. Drenol must be missing his family and that's why he's sad. I decide I'll go and make friends.

I cross the village, sliding down the slippery path to one of the center huts, where all the elders live together. Drenol is sitting in front of his hut, scowling as Jo-see and Haeden and Joden wander around with baskets. They're bringing little treats to everyone, and they already came by Mommy's hut. Drenol looks mad.

I approach him cautiously. He's sitting on a big rock in front of the hut and shifts his butt every few seconds. It must still hurt.

"Hi Drenol," I say.

"Go away." He doesn't even look at me, just scowls at Jo-see and Haeden, who are a few huts down.

I ignore that, remembering what Mommy said about Elly. *These things take time.* "Don't be sad," I tell him. "They'll come to your hut soon."

"Bah," he says. "They are fools."

"Why?"

"Because we should be careful with food." He glares at me. "When I was your age, we only ate one meal a day in the brutal season, because we had to make sure it would last."

Oh. "Which meal?"

"What?" He squints.

"Which meal is it?" I sit down near him, curious. "My favorite meal is breakfast cuz Mommy makes me eggs. They're from dirt-beaks, but they're not dirty like the dirtbeaks are because of the shell, so they're safe. That's what Mommy says, but she still washes the shell over and over again just in case."

Drenol shakes his head. "When I was your age, we did not eat eggs. You steal the young from their mothers. That is a terrible thing."

"Really? Mommy says they'll just lay new eggs. They don't even notice."

He leans in and glares at me. "Your mother is *wrong*."

I blink, fighting back the urge to cry. He's such a meanie.

Drenol shifts on his butt again, groaning, and then shakes his head. "Everyone in this tribe is foolish." He looks over at Jo-see and Haeden, and then sees them coming towards us. Then, he waves at me quickly. "Give me your shoulder."

I hop to my feet and move close, and he leans heavily on me, getting to his feet with a creak of bones. He sucks in his breath like I do when it hurts, and then shuffles into his hut.

I look over at the others heading this way. I think he's hiding from them. Should I tell him Jo-see is too fat with kit to play hide-and-seek? I follow him into his hut.

His fire is really low and it's cold and dark inside. As I watch, he shuffles over to his furs and throws one around his shoulders. He wouldn't need to cover up so much if he took care of his fire, so I move toward it and spear a cake of fuel from the fuel basket, and then toss it onto the coals, stirring them to bring more heat just like Papa showed me.

As I do, I look around. I've never been inside the elders' hut, and Drenol moves to a corner and lies down on his nest of furs, and in his area are baskets. Not just any baskets, but baskets with colors and patterns. He's got an old dvisti skull that's been colored all kinds of neat shades, too, with swirls and pretty designs on it. And in another basket...there's all kinds of carvings of animals.

They look like toys and I'm excited. The one on top looks just like a snow-cat. "Did Aehako make those for you?"

He gives me an irritable look. "I made those."

"Did you paint, too?"

"No, my mate was the painter. Are you going to keep asking me questions?"

"Do you want me to make you some tea?" I ask, ignoring his bad mood like Mommy said. She must be right, his butt must hurt him a lot.

"No."

I move toward the basket of carvings, because they look so neat. "These are really good."

"I know."

"The paintings are pretty, too. Did you paint them?"

"My mate did," he says proudly. "She would paint and I would carve by the fire at night."

"I like your carvings," I tell him, feeling shy. "Mommy is good at all kinds of things, but I'm too little to do carving myself."

"Bah. I was your age when I learned."

"Wow, then you've been doing this for a really, really long time."

He glares at me. "Are you saying I am old?"

"You're not?"

Drenol just sighs and shakes his head. "Kits."

I can't help but stare at the basket full of carvings. There's so many of them, and they're all tiny and lifelike. I see one that looks just like a metlak holding a baby on its back and my fingers itch to touch it. "You made these to play with?" I touch one hesitantly.

"No. I made them for my son, but he died."

"That's sad." I pull back, not wanting to touch them if it bothers him, but they're so good. "Can you show me how to carve like this?"

He's quiet, and I look over at him again. He's sitting up in bed. His expression is weird, like he can't decide if he's sad or angry.

Then he shakes his head. "Go away. My backside aches."

Drenol lies down and puts his back to me.

I leave, but my head is full of thinkings. I don't think he wanted to lie down so early or stay in his hut when it's so nice outside, but his butt hurts him. I think of the pretty painted things in his hut, and the carvings. Drenol likes special things. And I think of how much he talked even though he acted like he didn't want to.

Mommy's right. He's just sad and lonely. I didn't see any No-Poison gifts either. I bet he didn't get any because his mate and son are gone.

Someone should make him a gift. Everyone deserves something for No-Poison.

I race back home. "Mommy! Mommy!"

She's rolling her spindle against her leg, excitement on her face. "Look, Lukti! It's making yarn! I figured it out! I can make yarn and then we can make real fabric!"

"Okay," I say, trying to be excited for her. I move to her side and touch her other knee. "Mommy, I need you to help me make a present for Drenol cuz he doesn't have anyone."

She holds her spindle for a second, then puts it aside and pulls me into her lap, squeezing me into a great big hug. "You're a sweetheart, you know that, baby?"

I just giggle, because I'm ticklish. "Does that mean you'll help me?"

"Of course. What do you want to do?"

DRENOL

I nap for most of the day, because there is nothing else to do when you are old and your bones hurt. Vadren and Drayan are staying with the others as the festivities continue, so I am here alone.

That suits me fine. I need no company. It is quieter without the nattering of others. I can hear my own thoughts. I can sleep.

Again, I guess.

The fire is close to dying once more, but I do not have the energy to get up and stir the coals, not when it is just me here in the hut. It grows dark outside and I can hear distant laughter as others continue to feast and celebrate, but hearing that just makes me tired. My Koloi would have liked all the gift-giving, I think.

Someone scratches politely at the entrance to my hut, even though the screen is ajar.

"What?" I call, irritated. "I am not walking over there just because you are too shy to come in."

"It's me," calls a young voice. The boy from earlier. Lukti.

My heart aches. There is something about his eager gaze that reminds me of my young son, gone all these turns ago. Seeing him is painful. "What do you want?"

"I brought you a gift."

Eh? I sit up, curious. "A gift?"

The small head peeks around the corner and then Lukti comes into my hut. He carries one of the things humans call a "pillow," and it is nearly as big as he is, the stuffing thick. It is trimmed with white fur on the edges and is so large it makes him waddle, and outside I see his dark-skinned mother smiling with approval as he comes inside.

"Why do you think I need that?" I ask, struggling to get to my feet.

"It's for your butt," he calls out cheerfully. "So you don't hurt when you sit on your rock outside."

"We even made a strap," his mother adds. "So you can put it over your arm and take it with you around the village."

Lukti stands there, holding the pillow and smiling at me uncertainly. Angry words rush to my tongue, but then I pause, because in each corner of the pillow, I can see where he has sewn a decorative stitch in bright red—and the swirling design is one that Koloi painted all over the skull that sits next to my bed.

Clever, thoughtful boy.

"Well," I say, managing to straighten to my full height. "Let us try it out, then."

Excited, Lukti skips out to the front of the hut and I follow behind, much slower. His mother waits a short distance away, her arms crossed under her teats as she watches, a little smile on her face.

I move to my sitting rock and ease my weight down on the puffy thing. To my surprise, my tailbone is cradled perfectly and does not shoot fire up my back. "Well," I say again. "Your mother is very thoughtful."

"Oh no," she says. "This was all Lukti. I just helped."

I look down at the small, eager boy and nod slowly. "Then I thank you."

He beams at me, happiness wreathing his face and my chest aches. I reach out and pat his shoulder, and he comes and sits next to me on the big rock. "Mama says I can hang out with you if you want, and we're gonna have snow-cat stew at our hut if you want to come over for dinner later. She says no one else is gonna be there, just us, and your pillow will fit on a sitting rock there, too." The words rush out of him, as if he is afraid I will scowl him into silence before he finishes.

"Only if you want to," Teef-nee calls out. "No pressure."

"That is...very kind of you." I shift my weight on the pillow. Very comfortable. The thoughtfulness of this small kit is astonishing. "I thought I would stay here, but..."

"Stay here and carve animals?" Lukti asks, his voice full of excitement.

I was going to sleep since there is nothing else to do, but I do not tell him that. "You like the carvings that much?"

"Oh yes." His eyes shine with enthusiasm.

I gesture inside the hut. "Bring the basket and the leather wrap next to it that holds my tools." I nod at his waiting mother. "I will bring him home before dinner."

She winks at me and then strolls away as Lukti dashes into the hut.

The boy returns a moment later, his arms full of the basket of carvings and my tools. I point at the wrap. "Unroll that on the ground and I will show you what each tool is for. A good carver needs many different ones. See that big carving on top? Of the skyclaw?"

Lukti immediately grabs it and holds it up.

"You can have that one." I am rather proud of it, because the folded wings turned out well.

His eyes widen and he clutches it to his chest. "Really?"

"Really," I say, and then gesture that he should sit down in front of me. "But if you really want to learn, I can teach you..." And I am oddly pleased when he thumps to the ground in front of me, all eagerness and attention. "All right, then. See that first stick there? With the hard edge? That is your pick..."

THE END

THE ICEHOME SERIES

LAUREN'S BARBARIAN

A lush, tropical island on an icy planet makes no sense. Then again, not much makes sense anymore after waking up and finding myself not in bed but on a strange world populated by aliens. Here, I no longer need my glasses to see...which is good, because I'm far too busy staring at a sexy, four-armed alien named K'thar...

VERONICA'S DRAGON

Everyone expects resonance to happen when twenty newcomers are dropped onto the frosty world...and no one expects the gorgeous, golden god named Ashtar to resonate to someone like me, though. He's fierce. Flirty. Powerful. Disgustingly handsome. I'm...not any of those things.

But resonance seems to think we'd be great together. And Ashtar does, too...

WILLA'S BEAST

Beast. Creature. Monster.

Dangerous.

All of these things have been said about Gren.

Willa doesn't believe it, though. She knows that monsters can sometimes come in appealing packages. She knows that for all of his snarls and fearsome appearance, he'd never hurt her.

She's going to save him...or fall in love. Maybe both. Willa doesn't mind that he's a beast, as long as he's *her* beast.

(Looking for Ice Planet Barbarians? Oh, my sweet reader, let me introduce you to an entire series of big blue men...)

WANT MORE?

For more information about upcoming books in the Ice Planet Barbarians, Fireblood Dragons, or any other books by Ruby Dixon, 'like' me on Facebook or subscribe to my new release newsletter.

If you want to talk barbarians on Facebook, there's also a fan group called Blue Barbarian Babes who love to discuss everything on the ice planet! I'd love it if you check them out.

Thanks for reading!

<3 Ruby

Manufactured by Amazon.ca
Bolton, ON

31615370R00060